Death By Derby
A Josiah Reynolds Mystery

Abigail Keam

Worker Bee Press

ISBN 978 0 9906782 1 2

The history is true.
The historical horses were living flesh.
The horses in the Kentucky Derby race sequence
were all past Kentucky Derby winners.
Persian Blue and Comanche are names of Thoroughbreds
from the past and we pay homage to them in this story.
The artists are real, but the art may not be.
The characters are not based on you,
so don't go around town and brag about it.
Josiah Reynolds does not exist except in the author's mind.

Published in the USA

Worker Bee Press
P.O. Box 485
Nicholasville, KY 40340

Abigail Keam

Acknowledgements

The author wishes to thank Al's Bar, which consented to be used as a watering hole for my poetry-writing cop, Kelly.

Thanks to my editor, Heather McCurdy and Patti DeYoung.

Special thanks to Sarah Moore and Anna Lowery.

Artwork by Cricket Press
www.cricket-press.com

Book jacket by Peter Keam
Author's photograph by Peter Keam

Prologue

Charlie Hoskins was a self-made man. He had been born into poverty in the Appalachian Mountains near where Jenny Wiley had been taken captive by the Indians in the eighteenth century. In fact, he was a descendant of hers.

Born poor as a church mouse, Charlie pursued his education with relentless single-mindedness, and once he received his BA from Murray State University, he pursued the accumulation of wealth with the same determination. He was relentless in his pursuit of money, to such an extent he was universally hated.

Oh, he was admired for his rags-to-riches story. He was admired for being a good businessman. But Charlie never learned tact and made many enemies in the process of realizing his goals. He didn't care that in order to accomplish his dreams, he trampled on those of others.

The reason most of us in the Bluegrass didn't care for larger-than-life Charlie Hoskins was that he was a major developer in the area. Charlie seemed bent on buying every horse farm he could get his hands on and paving it over with concrete for another of his strip malls and housing developments. Many of his storefronts lay empty and barren, but that didn't seem to deter Charlie from building. He kept on and on, destroying some of the most precious farmland in the country in order to put up a parking lot.

Remind you of Joni Mitchell? If you don't know to which song I am referring, then you are not a child of the sixties or good protest music.

Charlie didn't care what people thought of him. Folks hadn't helped his family when they were down and out in the mountains, so he didn't care for their goodwill now.

But what Charlie did care about was that his Thoroughbred, Persian Blue, win the Kentucky Derby.

And next he cared about making a grand entrance in his hot air balloon on live television. He was going to land his balloon right in the infield. Charlie was determined to be as well known as Donald Trump, his hero, and his entrance at the Kentucky Derby would be his introduction to the nation.

Charlie didn't seem to mind that Churchill Downs would forbid it. He hadn't asked them. He would just pay whatever fine he received and beg for forgiveness after he gave Churchill Downs a large donation following his reckless stunt.

Yes, Charlie had determined he was going to be a household name, no matter whom he rubbed the wrong way.

Abigail Keam

1

I was just leaving Shaneika at Comanche's stall, when I spied a hot air balloon drifting overhead.

Shaneika and I watched it float past, wondering who was flying a hot air balloon so close to Churchill Downs on the day of the Kentucky Derby.

Then I saw Charlie Hoskins' name on the balloon.

"You've got to be kidding," complained Shaneika.

We looked at each other with disgust and then parted. I was going to get dressed in my finery, which included my new Derby hat, and join Lady Elsmere in her suite at Churchill Downs.

Shaneika and her trainer, Mike Connor, would go to her box to watch the Derby race, which was still hours away.

I hadn't gone more than several steps when I heard a loud boom! Looking up, I saw a fireball in the sky with charred debris falling to the ground. I suddenly realized that the balloon had exploded and its gondola was plummeting to the ground.

I quickly muttered a prayer, "Oh, God, please don't let anyone be hurt."

Turning, I searched for Shaneika.

She stood rooted, watching the burning wreckage fall to the ground.

Within seconds pandemonium broke out. Screams erupted from the track and horses neighing as they tried to bolt. People were running to safety, trying to dodge the flaming debris from the balloon.

I blinked several times, trying to order my thoughts. Did I really just see a hot air balloon explode in the air? And if I had seen what I thought I had seen, had Charlie been in the balloon and fallen to his death?

I looked back at Shaneika. This was terrible. If Charlie had been in that balloon, it wouldn't be long before the police would come to interrogate Shaneika.

Only several nights ago, Shaneika and Charlie had had a heated argument, and she had threatened Charlie in front of witnesses at Lady Elsmere's Derby party.

Shaneika stared back at me.

I could tell she was thinking the same thing as I was.

Shaneika might be in big, big trouble.

2

Charlie was not very popular with us—"us" being the Tates Creek clan—Lady Elsmere, Shaneika, Mike Connor, Velvet Maddox, Franklin, Matt, and me.

Shaneika had had run-ins with Charlie's staff over Comanche, not only during Derby week but at other tracks too. His boys were always standing too close to Comanche's stall or following Shaneika around the stables, deliberately bumping into her or whispering nasty things when they passed. Even though Shaneika had made a complaint against Charlie, the harassment continued.

Mike and Malcolm, the trainer and groom/hot walker, were watching Comanche like hawks. But still, the harassment continued. One day Mike found a farrier's nail in Comanche's feed.

Shaneika called for reinforcements, so I came days before the Derby to help out where I could and try to keep her calm.

"Charlie's people are trying to intimidate me," confided Shaneika.

I could see that she was unnerved by the harassment. Her usual support system was not present. Her mother, Eunice Todd, was in Versailles taking care of Shaneika's son, Lincoln. They probably would not see Shaneika until Derby Day on Saturday.

"Charlie must think Comanche is a threat to Persian Blue," I replied, trying to put a good spin on Shaneika's fears. "I can't believe that the racing authorities did nothing when you complained."

I was going through a bucket of oats to make sure nothing foreign was in the food and looked up occasionally as I was talking. Satisfied that the oats were sabotage-free, I gave them to Comanche or tried to.

In true Comanche style, he nipped me, or the hand that was *trying* to feed him. I really didn't like that horse. He was too feisty.

Mike put his arm around Shaneika. "Don't worry, Shaneika. I put in a call to Velvet. She'll be here to calm Comanche. He's picking up on your nervousness. That's why Charlie's trying to upset you. Horses are sensitive to emotions."

I chimed in, "And we are here. Everything will be fine. It's only a couple more days to the Derby. There's Lady Elsmere's party on Thursday. Let your hair down a little. Enjoy yourself. Pat yourself on the back, Shaneika. How many people get this far in racing? That in itself makes you a winner."

"Josiah is right, Shaneika. Relax. I've pulled some men from Lady Elsmere's farm to guard Comanche around the clock from now on. You don't need to worry."

I could see the tension in Shaneika's face drain away. I wondered if it was due to the fact that more guards were coming or that Mike was taking charge.

I was happy that Mike was here. I thought he was a good man and his presence calmed the tightly coiled spring that was Shaneika.

But neither of us knew that Mike was going to be the reason Shaneika and Charlie would get into a fight at the Derby party, or that it would escalate into such an ugly scene in front of so many people.

But when you threaten someone and then he dies in a spectacular accident, you can expect the police to knock on your door.

And knock the police did.

3

Let me explain this story as best as I remember it. If I jump around in telling it, stay with me. It will all make sense in the end.

My name is Josiah Reynolds. You say that's a funny name for a woman. I guess it is. My grandmother had a thing for kings in the Bible and thus was I named.

As to my vocation, I was an art history professor. Now I am a keeper of honeybees.

I became a beekeeper after my husband left me. Besides leaving me in body, he also left me broke both spiritually and financially. A triple whammy.

Brannon, my husband, hid his money and bequeathed an insurance policy to me. That was all. He gave the rest to his mistress, Ellen Boudreaux. Then he had the nerve to up and die on us both.

Brannon's money is legally mine, but I can't prove in a court of law where or how he concealed the money.

He must have hidden it in a Caribbean account. I never could trace it, but Miss Ellen sure was living in high cotton while I struggled to make ends meet. Well, that is until I got a settlement from the City of Lexington. I've been living much easier since then, but what a way to get some dough. I had to almost die to get it.

It all started when a man named Richard Pidgeon was found face down in my beehive–dead! The lead cop, Fred O'nan, investigating the case, had a grudge against me and tried to pin the man's murder on me.

In reality, Richard Pidgeon beat his wife, and she killed him in retaliation. She was the one who really tried to pin her husband's death on me. The crazy cop, O'nan, just took advantage of the situation.

So, to make a long, dreary story short, O'nan tried to kill me by pulling me off a cliff. I landed forty feet down on a ledge. I won't go into detail about my injuries, but I was banged up pretty badly. I now wear a hearing aid, smile with all new teeth, walk with a bad limp, and sport lots of ugly scars.

I came very close to death. Very close.

I decided to retaliate in my own way and made the city pay dearly for letting a crazy cop run wild. To their credit, they paid up.

I now spend my time working my bees and continue to get better each day by sticking to an extensive workout. Such a bore. The workout–not the bees.

So how do I fit into the current story? I happened to be a witness to all the important events.

Just my luck, huh?

I first met Shaneika Mary Todd when my daughter hired her as a criminal lawyer to protect my rights, when police were circling because of Richard Pidgeon's death several years ago. She kept the police at arms length until O'nan, the crazy cop, went ballistic. And then she sued the city for me. Somewhere during the process, we became friends.

Due to her passion for Thoroughbreds, Shaneika purchased ten acres from me and bought that eating and pooping machine, Comanche.

Then I met her mother, Eunice, and we went into business together. I let her use my house, the Butterfly, for tours and weddings. I help out where I can. After expenses, we split the money fifty-fifty.

As for Shaneika's namesake, Mary Todd Lincoln, let's say she stays mum. The Todds were a famous Southern family who owned slaves.

White owners sometimes crossed the slave racial and class barrier either due to love or evil intent, so many slaves were related by blood to their owners. This is still a sticky subject, which most Lexingtonians won't discuss.

Shaneika goes to all the white Todd family reunions, so that should tell you something. She has handwritten letters and artifacts from prominent nineteenth-century figures, including Abraham Lincoln, members of his cabinet, and Confederates, such as Jefferson Davis, decorating her office.

She is on the board for the Mary Todd Lincoln House, which is now a museum. Most of all, she wears original couture–like Chanel, Halston, Givenchy and carries vintage handbags–girlie accoutrements that you and I would kill for, which she says are handed down in her family.

In order to understand someone like Shaneika Mary Todd, you have to understand Lexington. And in order to get to the heart of Shaneika's story, you have to understand Bluegrass culture, which revolves around horses.

4

Winston Churchill once said, "There is something about the outside of a horse that is good for the inside of a man."

Humans love horses. We think of them as noble creatures, worthy of our love and respect. The names of horses like Seabiscuit, War Admiral, Man o' War, Secretariat, and Affirmed are burned into our brains. We cherish companion horses like Roy Rogers' Trigger, Dale Evans' Buttermilk or Gene Autry's Champion. Who doesn't know the cry of the Lone Ranger as he urges his gleaming white steed into action? "Hi-Yo, Silver!"

History even recorded that Alexander the Great's beloved black stallion was Bucephalus.

And of course, there is Mr. Ed. *"A horse is a horse, of course, of course. And no one can talk to a horse of course. That is, of course, unless the horse is the famous Mr. Ed."*

Did everyone sing along?

Let's continue.

How many times did your parents read *My Friend Flicka* or *Black Beauty* to you as a child? And who didn't get a tear in their eye when the pony died in *The Red Pony* by John Steinbeck?

We may not be interested in horse racing as our favorite sport, but most Americans will check to see who won the Kentucky Derby the first Saturday of each May.

So let's go back to the beginning–not Shaneika's beginning, but horse racing in general.

The reason horse racing is the heart of the Bluegrass is due to the geology. Underneath the lush grass, antebellum mansions, and rows of rolling fields filled with Thoroughbred, Standardbred, or Saddlebred horses, is a layer of limestone rich in phosphate and calcium. These two minerals nurture the soil from which grass grows and produces animals with very strong bones.

Still with me?

Now the type of grass is special too. It is a grass from the Old World that old timers say was brought by a settler accompanying Daniel Boone. When it is allowed to grow to its full height, it has a bluish gray tint when it moves in the wind. Thus its name–blue grass and the name stuck for the region–Bluegrass.

A little known fact is that ninety percent of the Bluegrass seeds are cultivated in Idaho, Oregon, and Washington, but I digress.

Prior to 1980, there were one hundred seventy-five horse farms in the Bluegrass. Horse racing and breeding were controlled by wealthy families who loved the sport of racing. Although they needed to break even on their expenses, money was not the object of the game for many. They coveted winning and the glory that went with it.

However, in the '80s, "new money" moved into the Bluegrass and gobbled up horse farms whose owners were not able to cope with the times. Now there were over four hundred horse farms covering fifteen counties and four thousand square miles. The emphasis on raising horses to win races now changed to making money on breeding rights.

Outrageous fortunes were gambled on breeding famous stallions to mares.

A prime example of a fortune gained and then lost due to mismanagement and possible corruption was Calumet Farm whose owners owned Alydar.

Calumet Farm, purchased with money from the fortune of the Calumet baking powder company, owned by the Wright family, was the premier Thoroughbred farm in the world. Located on Versailles Road outside of Lexington proper, its white fences and rolling emerald pastures were home to more winners than any other farm in racing history. It was the jewel of the Bluegrass racing industry. At least it was until it fell into the hands of those who looked upon horses as commodities.

Shares were sold for the right to breed with Alydar, which made Calumet Farm one of the wealthiest horse businesses in the world, but then something odd happened.

Alydar died under mysterious circumstances.

Soon, lawsuits and accusations of mistreatment of horses, embezzlement, and insurance fraud fell upon Calumet's managers and associates, causing the downfall of this great horse empire. At the end, Calumet had to be sold and all the wealth it had accumulated was gone forever.

The story of Calumet is a cautionary tale of greed, but there is a silver lining.

Calumet was saved from the bulldozer by Henryk de Kwiatkowski, a Polish immigrant to Canada, who made his fortune through the leasing and brokering of airplane sales. He purchased Calumet and its seven hundred seventy acres at a liquidation auction for a mere seventeen million.

Thank goodness.

I love the Bluegrass. When I drive down Tates Creek Road and see the mares and their foals grazing in the green pastures of horse farms, everything is right with the world. I see history in those horses. I see unspeakable beauty. I see land fought over by Native Americans and Europeans for the right to walk upon its sacred soil.

So you can understand why I get hot under the collar when I see these horse farms bought and paved over for a stupid shopping mall or a fast food joint.

Come on. Most of these tacky housing developments and malls are built by outsiders, who don't give a damn about this area. They are destroying one of the most fragile and unique places on earth. And the various county zoning boards in the Bluegrass are letting them. Why? Greed.

If I see one more *Growth Is Good* bumper sticker, I'm going to vomit. Literally.

And Charlie Hoskins was one of the destroyers, only he was one of our own—a born and bred Kentucky boy.

That just made it worse.

5

You need to know a little more about the horses that are bred in Kentucky before we can continue with our story.

Thoroughbreds race around an oval course, called a racetrack, with a small person called a jockey on their backs. The horse that completes the track first wins.

The Triple Crown for Thoroughbreds is the Kentucky Derby, the Preakness, and the Belmont races. Horses that win the Triple Crown are very expensive and very rare.

Saddlebreds were originally called Kentucky Saddlers and used as officers' mounts in the Civil War. They are show horses prized for their three-gaited and five-gaited strides. They do not race. They perform in a ring. Their Triple Crown is the Lexington Junior League Show, the Kentucky State Fair World's Championship Show, and the American Royal Show.

Standardbreds are horses that race around a track with a driver sitting in a sulky. They do not run. They trot.

Their Triple Crown is the Yonkers Trot, the Hambletonian Stakes, and the Kentucky Futurity.

Of course, these are American races for glory, money, and silver trophies. Other countries have their own shtick going.

All three breeds can trace their ancestry from Arabian horses, then to Britain, with final tweaks in America.

Shaneika's horse, Comanche, is a Thoroughbred and slated to compete in the most famous Thoroughbred race in the world–the Kentucky Derby!

I don't care for Comanche very much. He's lazy, cantankerous, and foul tempered. The only people that he allows near without trying to nip them are Shaneika and her son, Lincoln. And the fact that he is unusually difficult is fodder for the gossip circuit among the jockeys who make their living riding difficult and powerful horses. Shaneika always has trouble finding suitable jockeys who will take Comanche on.

Did I mention that he is eating Shaneika out of house and home?

Every dime she had has been invested in this eating machine called a racehorse. She even mortgaged her home.

Her mother, Eunice, told me in hushed tones one afternoon that Shaneika will be on the verge of bankruptcy if Comanche doesn't win the Derby.

Shaneika surely has racing fever.

Even though Comanche had made enough stakes money to enter the Kentucky Derby, I just didn't think he had it in him to win the coveted race.

But obviously Charlie thought he did. Otherwise, why would he bother to rattle Shaneika's cage?

6

Mike ran over to us after the explosion. "Are you okay?"

Shaneika and I both nodded, still stunned.

"What happened?" I asked. "Was it a stunt?"

"I don't know, but I will see what the hell is going on after I check Comanche," replied Mike, opening Comanche's stall door. "Whoa there, boy. Take it easy now."

"I haven't taken my eyes off him, Mike," reassured Shaneika. "I didn't step away during the explosion. No one could have gotten to him."

I stared at both of them. So they thought the explosion might have been a tactic to lure us away from Comanche's stall. Even though security was tight, unsavory things have been known to happen to a horse before an important race.

"What about his water?" asked Mike, rubbing his forehead in exasperation.

"I got his water myself while Josiah and the vet were with him."

"Comanche has been protected the entire time. He was never out of our sight and no one had access to him without one of us watching," I concurred.

"Did Velvet come by this morning?" barked Mike. I could see that he was more nervous than Shaneika. Shaneika nodded. "She said he was ready to race."

Mike nodded, obviously satisfied.

"Did you see the balloon exploding?" I asked. "What happened?"

Mike checked Comanche's legs and then pulled his head down to check the horse's eyes and muzzle. "Be good now, boy. You can eat after the race." Mike looked at us. "Nobody has given Comanche something to nibble, not even a treat like a carrot or peppermint?"

Shaneika and I shook our heads.

"Good. Good."

Malcolm, who also doubled as the hot walker and groom, raced over to us. "Did you see that balloon blow up? I was getting a sandwich and boom . . . what a noise it made." He handed us bottles of water. "Shaneika, your mama is here with Lincoln. They're eating in the dining room if you want to join them."

"I'm too nervous to eat. I'll call them and let them know I'm staying with Comanche."

"I think you should go with Josiah," cautioned Mike. "Like you said, you're nervous. Not good for Comanche. You go on now. It's still hours 'til the race. Malcolm and I have this covered."

"Malcolm, has your family arrived yet?"

"I talked to Gramp. They just got here."

"Is Lady Elsmere with them?"

Malcolm grinned. "When I called, Gramp was fighting with her Ladyship about sitting in a wheelchair. It would be easier to maneuver around the crowds if they could wheel her."

"Perhaps I better go help Charles with June. She can be a handful, especially when she wants to make a grand entrance," I suggested.

"I'll go with you. I need to change my clothes," commented Shaneika.

It was a long way from the barns to the clubhouse, so I waved down a Churchill Downs worker who was driving a golf cart and begged him to take us to the clubhouse. Thank goodness he was going that way.

Lady Elsmere had rented a suite where everyone could go when they wanted to relax. There would be food and drink in the suite as well as a place to wash horse slobber off our hands and change into our Derby finery, which included very large, expensive hats.

Shaneika and I arrived at the suite before Lady Elsmere's entourage, so we quickly changed our clothes, coiffed our hair, and managed to apply some makeup.

"Where's your wolf cane?" asked Shaneika. "I just now noticed that you're not using it."

"I think my walking has improved to the point that I'm not using it as often. But ask me again if I fall on my fanny."

"You've lost more weight."

I slid my hands down my dress. "Down to my college weight. Now we shall see if I can keep it off. It just helps my health if my weight is down. I guess after Brannon left, I ate out of loneliness. If I hadn't been so fat, I could have outrun O'nan. Maybe things would have been different for a lot of people," I replied wistfully, thinking of the number of people my fall had affected.

"Look!" cried Shaneika. "My hands are shaking from nerves."

"Let's go have a drink," I suggested. "I need one."

I wanted to make sure I got my fair share of booze, as the fans attending the Derby typically guzzle 7000 liters of bourbon and 120,000 Mint Juleps.

Shaneika nodded and as we began to leave the suite, a catering group that Lady Elsmere had hired barged in. Following them was Charles, pushing a wheelchair with a complaining Lady Elsmere balancing two champagne bottles in her lap.

Amelia and Bess pushed by the wheelchair and Charles, depositing their mother, Mrs. Dupuy, into a comfy chair by the window. Then they plopped down next to her, fanning themselves with racing programs.

"We couldn't get an elevator, so we had to walk up the steps," exhaled Amelia, breathing heavily. "Poor Mother!"

"I told her to get in a wheelchair like me," spouted Lady Elsmere, aka June Webster from Monkey's Eyebrow, Kentucky.

"I'm not old like you," retorted Mrs. Dupuy.

"Over sixty, everything takes a toll," replied Lady Elsmere.

"When I get to sixty, I'll let you know," sassed Mrs. Dupuy.

"I think water has gone over that dam," retorted Lady Elsmere.

Mrs. Dupuy started to reply when Charles cut her off, "Now ladies, hush. I can't hear myself think with all the noise from the stands and you two hens cackling."

Ignoring the fuss, I grabbed a bottle of champagne from Lady Elsmere's lap. "Hey, it's even cold," I announced to Shaneika.

"Can't you wait for lunch to have some of my very expensive champagne?" complained Lady Elsmere.

"No, June, we can't," I replied to Lady Elsmere. "We have had a tough morning and need a bit of the bubbly."

"Wouldn't have anything to do with Charlie's hot air balloon exploding, would it?" asked June, casting a steely glance at Shaneika.

"Oh, keep your eyeballs in your head, old woman," Shaneika shot back.

"Lady Elsmere is our hostess for the day," reminded Charles sternly.

I quickly poured a glass of champagne for Shaneika and handed it to her.

"I'm very sorry, Miss June. I'm so nervous I don't know what I'm saying. Please don't take offense."

Lady Elsmere smiled sweetly. "None taken."

"I think that's the first time you have ever offered an apology," I pointed out, looking at Shaneika in amazement. "And you goaded her," I accused June.

Lady Elsmere shrugged. "Just seeing what I could learn about the balloon explosion."

Charles grabbed the TV remote. "Let's turn on the TV and see what the news says about it," he suggested.

One of the caterers tugged at my elbow. "How should we address the lady in the wheelchair?"

I whispered back, "The public knows her as Lady Elsmere and her close friends call her June. We leave it at that."

"Oh," replied the young caterer, her eyes widening while taking in June and her glittering array of diamonds. "She's beckoning toward us. What does she want?"

"Your soul, I warrant." Looking at the young caterer's stricken face, I relented. "She wants you to take the other champagne bottle. I'll get it for you." I went over to June and grabbed the bottle out of her lap. "Be nice, June, you're scaring the help."

"One of life's little pleasures left to me."

"Oh really!" I looked around. "Where's Liam? Thrown him over for someone younger?" I asked, referring to Lady Elsmere's current paramour, who was an Irish grifter posing as a valet and lately turned into a sex toy for June's amusement.

"I think he's mingling with the crowd."

"Probably pickpocketing some poor schmuck."

"You're always thinking the worst of people, Josiah. It's unbecoming."

I gave June a knowing look. "Well?"

June sputtered, "If he does, I'll make sure he gives the loot back. Now let's enjoy this day. Charles, what does the boob tube say?"

Charles was listening to the sports announcer who was reporting that the races would continue. Apparently there had been an explosion and racing officials, firemen, and police were checking the damage, but all fires had been put out. No one was hurt and there was very little damage done to property so far.

Everyone sighed in relief.

"I thought they might call off the Derby," confided Shaneika, holding her stomach. Talk about a nervous cat on a hot tin roof.

I handed her my glass of champagne. "You need to drink more or take a Valium. You're overwrought."

"Overwrought? What a nineteenth century word!"

"Does it fit?"

"Yeah," she replied before downing the champagne. "Where can I get more of this?"

I beckoned to one of the caterers. "Don't go overboard with this stuff. You don't want to look like a lush on national television if Comanche wins."

"When Comanche wins," Shaneika replied emphatically.

"Okay, when he wins," I replied while mouthing to the head caterer to make lots of black coffee.

Shaneika swept away and sat next to June. "I'm sorry that Jean Harlow didn't win the Kentucky Oaks."

June nodded. "She did so well on her practice run, but in the race she faded after the second turn. I think I will switch jockeys when I take her to run in the Black-Eyed Susan Stakes."

"So you're going to Pimlico, then?"

"I must give Jean Harlow every opportunity to become a champion. She was bred for winning."

Before taking another sip of champagne, Shaneika asked, "After this year, what are your plans for Jean Harlow?"

"I plan to breed her with Comanche and get myself a Kentucky Derby winner."

Shaneika choked on her champagne until I patted her on the back. Yes, I was standing behind them eavesdropping.

"I refuse to die until my horse wins the Kentucky Derby," revealed June.

"Let's breed those two horses today then!" I mocked.

"Keep it up, Josiah, and you are out of my will," scolded June.

Shaneika laid her hand over June's gnarled ones. "I understand completely." She looked out at the racetrack. "For most people, it's about the money."

June interrupted, "But for you and me, it's about the glory."

"Yes," replied Shaneika wistfully. "It's all about the glory."

"You're still very young, but you will appreciate what I'm about to say. This is a man's business. Very few women have breached the cigar smoke and Kentucky bourbon of the Old Boys' Club to get this far. There was Penny Chenery, who owned Secretariat and Karen Taylor who owned Seattle Slew. Then there were a handful of women like Lucille Wright Markey and Fannie Hertz who owned horse farms, and Josephine Erwin Clay, the first lady to run a stud farm in the Bluegrass. She was the one that busted open the doors, but it's been hard for us gals to keep our hand in the game.

"Now there are you and me, plus a few others. We love our horses. We love the smell of the barn with its hay, leather, and manure. We love the smell of horse sweat. We love everything there is to love about this business, and I'm telling you, Shaneika, no one gives you anything. If you want to win, then you must take it.

"You let Charlie get to you. He was playing mind games at my Derby ball and you took the bait. Keep your mind on the next race and your horse. That's all that matters. Understand?"

"Yes, Miss June. I understand, and thank you for even considering breeding Jean Harlow with Comanche."

"He's got the stuff to become a winner, but he's got to believe it. I see him hesitating. You need to give him more room to stretch his legs. Keep your jockey from holding him back. Just let Comanche run the race his way."

I watched as both ladies whispered strategies and dreams, and wondered when I had been so enamored of a goal. I guess it had been learning to walk again. My, my, that had been a struggle.

I went into the bathroom and gazed into the mirror. It had been a long time since I had really looked at myself. Shocked at my appearance, I gingerly felt my face and then turned, scrutinizing my appearance.

My short hair was dyed a golden red, which went well with my pale skin. The hearing aid was well hidden and not noticeable unless one looked for it. My teeth, all implants, looked very American–that is straight and white. My face didn't look quite middle-aged yet, due to a little nipping and tucking when reconstructed. And yes, my body looked quite fit and muscular due to all the workouts.

I came to a conclusion. I was a fake. My hair was fake, my teeth were fake, my hearing was fake, and my face was unnaturally young for my years.

Some people would say that falling off that cliff was the best thing that ever happened to me due to my new look. But they didn't see the long, ugly scar running down my left leg or hear me cry when the pain got bad, as it still did. They hadn't witnessed the nasty scenes between doctors and me over pain medication.

What I would give for yellow teeth, crow's feet, and being fat if I could have skipped that horrible night when O'nan shot Franklin and Baby, and then pulled me off that cliff toward the dark, murky Kentucky River.

Shaneika stuck her head into the bathroom. "Wondered where you had wandered off to."

"I'm just putting on some lipstick," I fibbed.

"Some newscaster wants to interview me. Will you come? I would feel more confident."

"I'm surprised that you're nervous, Shaneika. You're such a bear in court."

"That's different. People are judging my client, not me. This interview is all about me. I don't know how to play this."

Smiling, I intertwined my arm with Shaneika's. "Remember this is your day, win or lose. You gave it your all. Be nice, but confident. If you need time to think just say, 'That's an interesting question,' or something like that."

"Sounds like a plan," replied Shaneika, pulling me along with her to the interview.

7

"How does it feel to be the first African-American to own a horse racing in the Kentucky Derby?"

I knew from the expression on Shaneika's face that she was remembering all the great black jockeys and trainers who had been forced out of American Thoroughbred racing due to Jim Crow laws starting in 1894. In fact, it wasn't until 2000 that Marlon St. Julien, an African-American jockey, rode in the Kentucky Derby after an absence of black jockeys for seventy-nine years.

The greatest jockey of all time is Isaac Murphy, the son of a slave, who won three Kentucky Derbies, and whose remains are buried next to Man o' War's at the Horse Park in Lexington.

"But I'm not. There was Dudley Allen, who owned Kingman, winning the Derby in 1891 and Byron McClelland with Halma in 1895."

I imperceptibly shook my head. This was not the time to launch into a diatribe on how the black man had been mistreated in horse racing.

The announcer blushed slightly for not doing his homework. He rushed to the next question. *"How does it feel to be the first African-American woman to win the Derby?"*

"I don't know. Comanche has to win it first."

Catching my frozen, wide-eyed facial expression, Shaneika put on her lawyer face and smiled at the camera, saying, *"It is an honor to be included in the Kentucky Derby whether Comanche wins or not."*

"Does it upset you that your horse is not considered a favorite?"

"I can only ask Comanche to do his very best. Of course, I want to win, but I consider this year at the Kentucky Derby the first of many years at the Derby."

"I'm sure that you are aware that a balloon owned by Charlie Hoskins exploded over Churchill Downs today. What are your thoughts on that?"

"I know very little about it. I hope no folks or horses were injured."

"There are rumors that you and Charlie Hoskins are having a feud? Any comment on that?"

Shaneika smiled. *"The entire racing community can be a contentious lot when racing against each other, but in the end we are a united brotherhood."*

"Do you think Charlie Hoskins' horse, Persian Blue, can beat Comanche?"

"As Persian Blue is the favorite, most people think he can beat my Comanche, but we will have to wait and see."

"Thank you, Shaneika Mary Todd, for speaking with us."
The announcer turned toward the camera. *"Shaneika Mary Todd, one of the few female owners in the racing business today and owner of the black steed, Comanche, on his chances of winning the Kentucky Derby.*

"There you have it, Ladies and Gentlemen, another historic first at the Kentucky Derby at the famed Churchill Downs."

I gave Shaneika a thumbs-up as she took off her microphone.

She thanked the announcer, and as we stepped out of the booth, two men stopped us.

One of the men flipped an ATF badge and demanded that Shaneika accompany them.

My heart froze as I grabbed Shaneika's arm. "Don't go with them!"

"What's the matter? You look like you've seen a ghost, Josiah!" questioned Shaneika.

"I HAVE!" I exclaimed, pointing to one of the men. "That man was Asa's husband! The one that double-crossed her!"

8

Shaneika put on her lawyer's face again. "May I have a closer look at your badges, please?"

Both men held up their badges.

Shaneika perused them slowly.

Holding my breath, I stupidly held on to the back of Shaneika's dress, afraid they might try to whisk her away. My eyes met the gaze of Asa's former husband.

His stare never wavered.

My heart pounded faster.

Satisfied that the men were actually from the ATF, Shaneika stepped back. "Were you Asa Reynolds' husband?"

"I was," answered a tall man in a Burberry coat, who flicked his eyes toward her.

"I consider your involvement to be a conflict of interest as Asa Reynolds and her mother are my clients."

"This isn't about Asa Reynolds," retorted the man, his facial expression and voice neutral.

"Then what's it about?" Shaneika asked, perplexed.

"We have some questions to ask you about Charlie Hoskins."

"I see," responded Shaneika thoughtfully. "It still is a conflict of interest. I'm afraid I can't talk to the two of you."

"Under the Patriot Act, we can force you to come with us."

"I hardly think a balloon accident comes under national security, especially if Charlie Hoskins had anything to do with it. I didn't realize that the ATF had a department covering stupidity.

"I have a race to watch. I will be happy to make an appointment with you on the day and time of your choosing but not today, gentlemen. Please excuse me."

My hand tightened around the fabric of her dress.

Shaneika walked around Tweedle-Dee and Tweedle-Dum with me clutching her dress and trailing behind.

We left the men huddled in a sad little pile of togetherness, but I could not stop shaking from fear.

9

When Shaneika and I arrived back at the suite, Shaneika's mother, Miss Eunice, and her son, Linc, had joined the group. As usual, Lincoln was stuffing his face and wearing Lady Elsmere's diamond and emerald bracelets.

Lincoln jumped up, spilling the plate on his lap. "Mama, you were great on TV."

"That's nice, Linc. Now give Miss June back her jewelry before you break it. I can't afford to replace those stones if they get loose from the settings."

"Aw, okay," whined Lincoln.

Eunice rose from her chair and went over to her daughter, kissing her on the cheek. "You looked very elegant, my dear. I'm very proud."

"Thank you, Mom. You know I better get down to the paddock. It's time to show Comanche off to the public."

"Sure, you go ahead. We'll meet you in the owner's box to watch the race."

"Make sure you're there."

"Baby, Linc and I will be waiting for you." Eunice smiled with pride. "I just gotta pull Lincoln away from all this food before he busts."

Always the perfect gentleman, Charles rose from his chair to escort Shaneika to the paddock.

I sat in Charles' seat.

"Whatever is the matter with you?" questioned June. "You're trembling."

I grabbed June's champagne glass and took a large swig. "You won't believe who I just saw."

"Well, don't keep me in suspense, especially at my age."

I could barely spit out the words, "Asa's ex-husband, Minor Reasor."

June reared back in shock. "I can't believe that he would show his face in Kentucky."

"Oh, June, it's worse than that. He's more handsome and arrogant than ever, and still working for the ATF."

"What's he doing here?"

"He wanted to interview Shaneika about Charlie Hoskins."

June thought for a moment. "The ATF does investigate explosions, and that balloon blow-up was a doozy. The news cameras didn't catch it, but many of the spectators in the infield taped it and now it's on every channel. No one could have survived it. It was horrible."

"And someone must have tipped off the ATF about the fight Charlie and Shaneika had at your Derby party."

"Still, how did he get here so fast? I have a bad feeling about this, Josiah. A very bad feeling."

"Shaneika wouldn't talk to them today, but she will have to talk with them eventually."

"Look, the next race is starting. We'll have to discuss this later."

I nodded and left the suite, looking for a pay phone. They were very hard to find in this day and age, but I finally found one. I dialed a number that I had memorized. When the line on the other end was answered, I just said one word, "Rosebud."

10

Minor Reasor checked into Louisville's historic Seelbach Hotel. All he wanted to do was shower and order room service. He was beat and dirty from the day's work. Part of it was spent on the crime scene and the other part was spent running down and interviewing witnesses.

He usually worked cases involving the smuggling of alcohol or tobacco. In fact, he had worked on breaking up Kentucky's notorious Cornbread Mafia, but that had been years ago.

The ATF had gotten a tip days ago that something was going to go down at Churchill Downs during the Derby, so he pulled in every favor to get assigned to the case. ATF and Homeland Security agents had been all over Churchill Downs for a week prior to that Saturday.

He had his own reasons to be here. It was to stir things up. Sometimes old wounds never heal.

Throwing off his tie and kicking off his shoes, Minor went into the bathroom and quickly disrobed. Taking a hot shower, he emerged wearing a thick cotton towel.

Then Minor stopped short.

Sitting in a chair was Asa Reynolds pointing his own gun at him.

"Hello Minor."

"How did you know I was here, Asa?"

"I remembered that you have always loved this hotel. It was simply a matter of having my people stake it out."

"Were you already in Louisville?"

"No."

Minor sat on the bed. "Ah, your mother must have called."

Asa didn't reply, but waved the gun at the door when someone knocked.

Minor twitched at the sound. "Your people again?"

Asa smiled. "I think it may be room service. I took the liberty of ordering for you."

Minor rose and answered the door.

True enough, it was room service. Minor signed for it and closed the door.

"Would you like to taste my food first?" questioned Minor with a lackadaisical grin.

"Don't worry," replied Asa. "It's not poisoned." She pinched a strawberry and ate it. "At least not by me."

She rose and put Minor's gun on the bed. "You shouldn't leave those things lying around. Never know who will pick them up. Someone might get hurt."

Minor lifted the covers off the dishes. "You remembered what I like to have after a case."

"Breakfast. Two eggs over easy, toast, stack of wheat pancakes with bacon and black coffee." She started toward the door. "I'll leave now. You need to eat before your eggs get cold."

"So soon? Why did you come?"

"To let you know that I'm around."

"Are you threatening me?"

"You wish. I'm just letting you know that I'm not the naïve, idealistic kid I once was. I know the score now."

"Gee, you troubled yourself to come here to say that."

Asa smiled. "I'll be watching you, Minor."

"It's illegal to interfere with the investigation of a case or threaten a law enforcement officer. I could have you arrested, Asa."

"Goodnight, Minor."

"Wait. Wait!"

But Asa was gone.

When Minor opened the door to his room and looked into the hallway, there was no sign of his former wife.

"How in the hell did she get away so fast?" he mumbled to himself as he shut the door.

He should have realized that Asa would be nearby.

In fact, Asa was three doors down, watching Minor chow down his pancakes. "Good work, Boris."

"It's easy to plant hidden cameras."

"He'll probably search the room after he's eaten and find them. He's no dummy. Just keep tabs on Minor. I want to know everything he does."

"Where're you going?"

"I'll get in touch when I'm needed. Minor has already called his boss to tell him I'm here. Within an hour, this hotel will be full of agents. Gotta go. I would advise you to do the same. You can watch him from anywhere."

Boris knew better than to argue.

Asa went through a connecting door to the suite and quietly slipped out through another exit into the hallway.

Boris gathered his equipment and headed downstairs. As he was hurrying out through the kitchen, a black SUV pulled up in front of the hotel.

Four men in dark suits climbed out and hurried inside the Seelbach Hotel.

11

"Why did you have to see Minor, Asa?" I asked.

"I wanted to rattle his cage some."

"And did you?"

Asa smiled as she looked over the cliff and across the river to the green rolling hills of Madison County. "Revenge is a tasty dish best served cold. However, I want to make him sweat a little bit first."

"Revenge is mine, sayeth the Lord," I quoted.

Asa finished the quote. "I will repay. In time their foot will slip; their day of disaster is near and their doom rushes upon them."

"Whosoever smites thee on thy right cheek, turn to him the other also."

Asa wistfully turned and looked at me. "Mom, you know my psych evaluation. I'm a sociopath. We don't turn the other cheek." She looked away from me. "We obliterate the threat."

12

"Ms. Todd, you can sit here. Thank you for coming."

Shaneika sat in the ATF office located in Louisville. "This is my lawyer, Richard Mandrake," she announced.

"Do you need a lawyer?"

"I want to make sure that nothing I say is misquoted or taken out of context."

"Can I offer you something to drink?"

Shaneika smiled. "No, and neither will my attorney have anything to drink or eat."

"I notice that you are wearing gloves?"

"Any law against that?"

"No, but it makes one wonder."

"Can we have your names and badge numbers, please?"

"Sure. I'm Agent Joseph Caperella and this is Agent Minor Reasor." Both ATF men pulled out their badges and let Shaneika take a snapshot of them.

"Being overly cautious for an 'innocent' person, aren't you?" questioned Agent Caperella, putting away his badge.

Shaneika placed a tiny tape recorder on the table and pushed the "on" button. "Let's get this over, shall we?"

Agent Caperella shrugged while glancing at Minor. "Okay, let's start."

"Name and address for the record, please."

Shaneika leaned across the table. "Let's cut the formalities. Why am I sitting across the table from two ATF agents?"

"We are investigating the balloon explosion at the Kentucky Derby. The ATF always investigates high profile explosions."

"Who owned the balloon and who was in it?" Shaneika demanded.

Minor shot back, "We ask the questions here. Not you."

Shaneika leaned back against her chair. "You know fellows, there are all sorts of things wrong with this interview. Number one—it is rumored that Charlie Hoskins owned the balloon. Now Charlie didn't have a lot of admirers. I would say that Charlie had lots of people holding a grudge or two against him. Out of all those people who didn't like Charlie, you seem to be honing in on a black woman. Are you interrogating lots of white people as well or just little ol' me?"

"This is not about race. This is about justice," assured Joseph Caperella.

49

Shaneika snorted. "Like the Ruby Ridge case?"

Both men twitched at the mention of Ruby Ridge.

"We're not here to discuss cases of the past. We're here to discover the how and why of the balloon explosion over Churchill Downs."

"Has the explosion been ruled as accidental?" asked Richard Mandrake, looking up from his notepad.

"We haven't reached a conclusion yet."

Shaneika started to say something, but Richard put his hand on her arm.

"So at the moment you don't know if the balloon blew up due to human error, incompetence, equipment failure, or tampering?"

Minor stated, "We're not saying where we are in this investigation."

"Then let me state this for the official record. My client, Shaneika Mary Todd, had absolutely nothing to do with the balloon explosion near Churchill Downs, nor does she know of anyone that does."

Agent Caperella started to interrupt but Richard Mandrake shut him down.

"Shush, shush. I'm not finished. We can prove beyond a shadow of a doubt that from Thursday night to Sunday, Shaneika Mary Todd was involved in Derby festivities. There are hundreds of witnesses plus video that will attest to that.

"Also, Agent Reasor, you shouldn't have been assigned to this case as you have a negative association with two of Ms. Todd's clients. Your superior should

have known better than to send you. I am sure it was
done intentionally, but it seriously compromises the case.

"I want you to know that tomorrow morning I am
going to file a complaint with the Department of Justice.
You all should know better. Really."

Richard Mandrake stood and clasped his leather case
shut. "Let's go, Ms. Todd. We've said all we're going to
say at the moment."

Minor stood and held open the door. "We'll be seeing
you," he pledged to Shaneika. "You can count on that."

"I better not, Agent Reasor. Ever," retorted Shaneika.

Richard Mandrake put himself between Minor and
Shaneika and escorted her out of the building.

Minor and Joseph sat down at the table. Joseph pulled
out a cigarette.

"No smoking in a federal building," reminded Minor.

"Like I give a shit," replied Joseph, lighting up. "What
are they going to do? Arrest me for smoking?"

Minor didn't reply, but silently thought that he had
made a mistake coming back to Kentucky.

13

"Tell me why Shaneika got into it with Charlie at June's Derby party," solicited Asa, sitting at my Nakashima dining room table.

I had to think back. "It started last racing season. As you know the horses have to make so much money at certain stakes races in order to be contenders for the Derby. Well, in two of them Comanche ran against Persian Blue and won. Then Comanche started losing and losing badly.

"Shaneika called in Velvet Maddox, the dowser, and Velvet found that a sponge had been shoved up Comanche's nose."

"That could have killed Comanche!" exclaimed Asa, incensed at the cruelty.

"Exactly. Comanche couldn't breathe properly and that's the reason he lost the races."

"What did Shaneika do?"

"Nothing. She couldn't prove that it was Charlie's doing, but Charlie was never one for keeping his ugly remarks to himself. He pissed many horse owners—not just Shaneika," I replied.

"But why focus on Shaneika? Is it because she's a black woman?"

I shook my head. "Oh, heavens no. It's because Comanche is a descendant of Eclipse and Persian Blue is not."

"Mom, I know that means something to you, but not to me."

"Eclipse was a horse in the eighteenth-century who passed on a genetic mutation of a very large heart to his daughters. Comanche's dam is from Eclipse's line."

Asa shrugged and looked inquiringly at me.

"Racehorses with extremely large hearts become champions because they can take in more oxygen while running. It improves their performance.

"During 1973 and 1974 Sham and Secretariat were two great Thoroughbreds competing against each other. Secretariat always won. His heart weighed twenty-two pounds while Sham's weighed only eighteen. Secretariat could run faster because his heart was more efficient."

"Surely there are other factors in a horse race."

"Oh, sure," I replied. "A horse has got to want to win, the jockey has to be good, but a very large ticker sure helps."

"Sooooo, tell me about Charlie and Shaneika," prodded Asa, cutting into a piece of strawberry-rhubarb pie Miss Eunice had made.

"I think Charlie was fearful of Comanche and since Charlie was Charlie, he was bent on unnerving Shaneika. She was an easy target. She was the only woman owner vying for the Derby this year. She was black. And she was mortgaged up to the hilt because of that horse."

"So what did he do?"

"He had his employees make suggestive remarks when they passed Shaneika at the stables or workouts. They hung around Comanche's stall to the point that Shaneika had to hire more people to guard Comanche 24/7. That's expensive."

Asa took a bite of the pie. "Oh, this is good pie." She wiped her mouth. "The crust is so flaky. Getting back to Shaneika, why didn't she file a complaint?"

"Don't talk with your mouth full of food, dear. She did and nothing came of it. Finally, she had to install expensive cameras and recording equipment. It slacked off some, but not all.

"The coup de gras came on the night of June's Derby party. Shaneika came with Mike Connor as her escort. They were having fun for once and really enjoying themselves. After all that hard work and sacrifice, Shaneika and Mike were finally relaxing."

Having eaten her slice of strawberry-rhubarb pie, Asa cut another piece.

"Leave me some," I complained.

Asa waved her fork. "Go on with the story."

"Charlie was standing with a group of people, yakking away when Shaneika and Mike danced past them. That's when all hell broke loose." I hesitated.

"Go on," urged Asa again.

"When Shaneika and Mike danced by, Charlie made the nasty remark, 'There goes a swirl'."

Asa put down her fork. "Oh, boy."

"Shaneika just snapped. She pulled away from Mike and got in Charlie's face. 'What do you mean by that remark, Charlie?' she said.

"Charlie gave her a stupid grin and said, 'What remark?' She should have known that he was baiting her, but her nerves broke and she went off, calling Charlie a racist bastard and telling him if he ever came near her again she'd cut off his balls and stuff them in his mouth."

Asa grinned.

"It's not funny, Asa," I insisted. "It was very embarrassing to witness, a very ugly thing for Charlie to say, and it ruined the party. June was miffed. Now Charlie's dead and the State Police, FBI, and the ATF are looking at Shaneika."

"We don't know that Charlie is dead. Nothing has been confirmed," countered Asa.

"Then where is he? Charlie would never miss Persian Blue running in the Kentucky Derby. Never."

Asa shrugged. "As far as we know, Charlie could be sunning himself in the Bahamas."

"You know something I don't?"

"What happened after Shaneika threatened Charlie?" asked Asa, ignoring my question.

"Mike pulled Shaneika away and they left, but not before I hurried after them to express my dismay at Charlie's remark. I found Shaneika crying."

"Crying!!"

I reaffirmed, "She was bawling like a little girl, a complete meltdown. Even Shaneika has feelings.

"The whole affair was just a mess. I think Mike is a good man, and he and Shaneika have gotten very close this past year. Just when things were looking like they might become even closer, Charlie has to make that stupid remark about Mike being white."

"Are you playing matchmaker, Mom?"

"Jumping Jehosaphat, the girl should have a love life. Shaneika needs a push. She knows Mike is good for her, but she holds back because he's white."

"Maybe she's skittish because he's a man. It might have nothing to do with Mike being white. Maybe she doesn't want to get involved with someone at this stage of her life. She's got a lot on her plate."

Hmmm, I thought. *This might be the time to fish for some information.* "No one ever talks about Lincoln's father. Not Eunice, not Lincoln, and certainly not Shaneika. I don't think his birth was due to an Immaculate

Conception. I have seen a picture of a handsome black man in her office."

"You're fishing," pointed out Asa.

"Yes, I am. Are you going to tell me anything? Do you know something?"

Asa rose with her empty plate and fork in hand. Bending over, she kissed the top of my head and then headed into the kitchen where she put the dirty dishes in the dishwasher. She then grabbed her jacket. "I have something to do. I'll be back before dinner."

"I know you know something," I called after her.

"Later, alligator," she remarked, heading toward the front door and waving goodbye.

I slumped in my chair. How was I going to help Shaneika if no one ever told me anything? I suddenly got an idea.

Maybe I would drop in at Al's Bar and see an old friend.

14

"May I sit down?" I asked my old buddy, Officer Kelly. I noticed that he was drinking bourbon.

Kelly looked up with bloodshot eyes. He seemed surprised to see me. "If you must," he replied, looking back down at his papers.

Ignoring the less than welcoming invitation, I sat down in a battered, duct-taped booth. Picking up his glass, I took a sip of his drink.

"Can I order you something?" he groused, taking the glass of bourbon away from me.

I motioned to the waitress. "Yeah, I would like two cheeseburger platters with fries and two diet cokes with a cup of black coffee. Bring the coffee now, please."

"I'll take another one of these," ordered Kelly, waving his bourbon glass.

I shook my head toward the waitress at that suggestion as I tidied up the table by combining all of Kelly's papers and stacking them in a neat pile.

"Working on a new poem?" I asked, giving them a quick perusal.

"Maybe."

Leaning over the table, I sniffed Kelly. He reeked. Scrutinizing him, I noticed his face was covered in stubble and his shirt looked dirty. "You haven't called me for months." I thought for a moment. "Since you came to see Asa at the hospital around Christmas time, I haven't heard a peep out of you. What gives?"

I had come to weasel some information out of Kelly, but now that I saw the condition he was in, information was the last thing on my mind. Something was very wrong.

Kelly winced.

"Kelly?"

He started to speak, but then clammed up when the waitress brought over his coffee. "I wanted another bourbon," Kelly complained.

"I've cut you off," I interceded as the waitress put down the cup.

Kelly began to gripe, but I interrupted, using the "mother" tone. "Shut up and drink the coffee. Miss, where's our food? I think we need it fast."

Sensing that an unpleasant scene might be brewing, she skedaddled into the kitchen.

Kelly took a sip of the hot coffee. "Tastes awful," he complained.

"Well, here's some cream. Drink up," I commanded. "Ah, here's our food." I poured ketchup on Kelly's plate and salted his fries the way he liked.

We ate in silence except for occasional encouragement from me to keep eating. Finally, we finished and I asked the waitress to clear our table. I noticed that the place was filling with regulars and the noise level had gone up. I could now talk to Kelly without the waitress overhearing our conversation.

"What's going on, Kelly?"

Kelly looked away and seemed reluctant to speak.

"I've known you since you were a boy. I feel like I've always been a second mother to you. Now give. I'm growing tired and my leg is starting to hurt. I'm running out of patience."

Kelly spread his hands out on the table. "My marriage is over," he said simply.

"What do you mean your marriage is over?"

"She kicked me out."

"How long ago?"

"Sometime in March."

"That long ago!" I exclaimed.

"She said I was moody. Too hard to get along with."

"That doesn't sound like you. Why were you like that?"

Kelly shook his head. "Reasons. Private reasons."

"Is she filing for divorce?"

Kelly shrugged.

"Is she filing for divorce, Kelly?"

"I don't know."

"What are you doing about it?"

He shrugged again. "What can I do? If she wants a divorce, then she wants a divorce."

I tried another tactic. "Okay. Let's go back to why you were so moody."

"Private reasons, I tell ya," Kelly shot back.

I leaned against the back of the booth and studied my friend. Something was very wrong here. I could tell he was suffering, but embarrassed to reveal the reason behind his suffering.

Grabbing my purse and then his papers, I climbed out of the booth. "Come on," I insisted, tugging on his arm.

"What for?"

"We're going to my house to get you cleaned up."

"NO!!"

"Kelly, you get your fanny out of that booth and follow me or I swear that I will get the good people at Al's Bar to literally pick you up and throw you into my car!"

Seeing that I was adamant and not going away, Kelly reluctantly scooted out of the booth and followed me–or I should say, staggered after me.

I got Kelly into my car and buckled him up.

I can assure you that it was very long drive home.

15

I got Kelly into bed. No, that's not right. I put a drunken Kelly to bed. Don't get any wrong ideas there.

Then I called Asa. She picked up on the first ring.

"Don't come home," I said. "Get a room at a hotel."

"Why?"

"Because I just put a soused Kelly to bed."

"Why's he drunk?" Asa asked.

"It might have something to do with the fact that his wife kicked him out of the house."

"Oh, that's not good!"

"My thoughts exactly. Just stay away while I clean up this mess you caused."

"Don't be mad."

"I'm not mad."

"Yes, you are."

"You're right. I'm furious. I warned you what could happen when you started up with Kelly again and now it's come to pass."

"I didn't mean for any unhappiness," she insisted.

"This is what happens when you don't listen to your mother."

I hung up.

16

After getting Kelly settled, I went back into town. I knew that Kelly would be asleep for hours and I had some free time.

Goetz answered his door. He looked surprised. "I thought our date was tomorrow night."

"It is, but I needed to see someone who wasn't about to throw himself off a bridge."

"Huh?"

"Nothing."

"I take it that it has been a rough day."

"Get me a drink, will ya?" I begged, sitting down on the couch and putting my feet up.

"Well, I was just about to go out," replied Goetz, looking sheepish.

"Really?"

"Yeah. I have a doctor's appointment."

"My own fault for barging in on you unannounced," I admitted. "Let me walk you out."

"You go on. I have to get some bills ready for the postman before I go."

I got up and grabbed my jacket before kissing Goetz on the cheek. "I'll see you tomorrow then."

"Seven on the dot."

"You've got the tickets?"

Goetz followed me to the door. "I've got the tickets. Don't worry. See you later."

I waved goodbye and hobbled my usual limp down the hallway to the elevator. Looking back, Goetz was standing in the hallway, watching me. He waved.

I waved back and as the elevator door opened, I got in, but only took it to the next floor. I waited a few minutes and then I took the elevator back up to Goetz' floor.

I know when I'm being hustled.

It would be interesting to see what he was up to and I didn't really care if Goetz caught me at it.

So I tiptoed back—not literally. That's a figure of speech as I can't tiptoe anymore, but you get the idea.

I put my ear against the door.

Oh my. What juicy tidbits I heard!

17

Minor Reasor emerged from Goetz' bedroom. "You're dating Josiah Reynolds?" he asked incredulously. "I always thought she was a fuddy-duddy."

"Many words come to my mind describing Josiah Reynolds but fuddy-duddy is not one of them. What are you . . . four?"

"She always seemed so stuck-up and provincial."

"I think hostile is a better word. She thinks you tried to frame her daughter."

Minor didn't reply. "Let's change the area under discussion."

"Touchy subject?" sneered Goetz.

Minor ignored Goetz' remark. "What have you heard?"

"I talked with my buddies who work at Churchill Downs and some of my gambling contacts. They say that a body wasn't found in the wreckage." Goetz watched Minor's expression.

"Do they give a reason why they say that?" asked Minor.

"Uh, because a body wasn't found. Not a foot or a hand or even a tooth. Nothing. Is it true? Nobody was in the gondola?" prodded Goetz.

Minor poured himself a drink and stared out the window. "Anything else?"

"No one saw Charlie at Churchill Downs on Derby Day and no one has seen him since."

Minor turned around. "He was seen getting in the balloon gondola at Bowman Field in Louisville. Spectators said the balloon took him straight up. So where did he disappear to between Bowman Field and Churchill Downs?"

"That's the sixty-four thousand dollar question," replied Goetz.

"No male of Charlie Hoskins' age or description has shown up anywhere. It looks like this whole explosion was staged and Charlie took a powder. And if he took a powder–why?"

"I have some thoughts on that."

"Which are?"

"This is information that I got from Josiah via Shaneika Todd. Charlie Hoskins was only part owner of Persian Blue and with only a small stake. In reality, he was a front man for a very large syndicate that planned to make a fortune on breeding rights to Persian Blue."

"That's taking a huge chance that Persian Blue would survive his races without getting injured. If hurt, the syndicate would have to refund stud fees to anyone who had already paid for breeding."

"According to Shaneika, Charlie had already paid the entry fees for the Preakness and Belmont, which is no chicken feed."

"So it was thought that Persian Blue had the stuff to be a Triple Crown winner," commented Minor.

"If he won just one of those races, his breeding fees would go up dramatically."

"If Charlie thought Persian Blue to be a contender, why would he jump ship?"

"I always say 'follow the money.' See if Charlie withdrew large amounts of cash before disappearing," advised Goetz

"Anything else?" requested Minor, looking out the window again.

"Not at this time."

Minor turned toward Goetz. "If Jo Reynolds left the building, hasn't she had time to get to the parking lot for her car?"

"What's that?" growled Goetz, hurrying to the window.

Both men peered out, wondering where I was.

18

Ooops!

They were on to me.

I knocked on the door.

There were muffled sounds of movement and then Goetz answered the door. His face was flushed.

"Hi again," he gushed, peering around me and glancing down the hallway."

"I forgot my purse," I said sweetly. I pushed by him and retrieved the purse that I had "accidentally" forgotten.

Goetz rubbed his hand through his thick hair. "I didn't even see it there."

"You ready?"

"Ready?"

"Ready to go to the doctor's office now. You can walk me down."

Goetz glanced at his bedroom door. "Yeah. I need to leave or I'll be late for my doctor's appointment." He reached for his coat.

"Don't forget your bills to mail," I reminded.

Goetz looked blank for a moment and then he remembered what he had told me. "Thanks," he mumbled. He grabbed some papers off his desk and stuck them in his pocket.

He then unceremoniously pushed me out the door, locking it behind him. "Come on. Let's go or I'll be late."

I admit I did my best to walk as slowly as I could, chattering all the way, while droplets of sweat broke out on Goetz' forehead.

I just love yanking his chain.

Aren't I a stinker!

Don't answer that.

19

"Are you sure it was Minor?"

"I think I'd know the voice of my former son-in-law."

Asa and I were sitting in the lobby of the Gratz Park Inn, tucked away in downtown Lexington.

"Shaneika filed a complaint against his boss for sending Minor here. She was told that Minor would be pulled from the case due to his connection with us," revealed Asa.

"Well, he's still around and having private conversations with Goetz."

"With your new boyfriend?"

"Don't be ridiculous. We're not a couple. We just do things together, you know, social things."

"That's what people call dating."

"WE ARE NOT DATING!" I yelled. Embarrassed, I looked around to see if anyone was watching.

Asa rested her teacup on her lap. "If you say so."

"Minor told Goetz that Charlie Hoskins was not in that gondola."

"There are witnesses who saw Charlie get into the gondola and the balloon lift into the air."

"Somewhere between Bowman Field and Churchill Downs, Charlie got out."

"Don't you think someone would have witnessed that? A person doesn't often see a huge balloon in their neighborhood. It's an object that cries for attention," said Asa.

"I'm just telling you what Minor told Goetz."

"Let's say that Charlie did get out of the balloon somehow. What would be the purpose of exploding it?"

"So people would think that he was dead."

Asa shook her head. "It would only take a few hours for the police to determine that no one was in the gondola. I don't see a real purpose there."

"Then what?"

"To provide a distraction. To create confusion. The police have never confirmed that a body was found. What if Charlie wanted to distract certain people with the explosion to allow time for him to get away."

"On Derby Day when his horse is running? Why would he do that?"

"Maybe he was desperate."

"He would have to be desperate to miss his own horse running in the most important race of the year."

"Something was more important than the Derby. We've just got to find out what." Asa thought for a moment.

"It has nothing to do with us, thank goodness." I got up to leave.

"Do you think I can come home tomorrow?"

"Call me. Right now Kelly is still sleeping it off. I'm going to see his wife. Maybe I can fix this."

Asa rose too. "Perhaps I should see her."

"Oh, goodness no. That would be throwing gasoline on the fire."

"Can I see Kelly?"

I stared at Asa. "Sometimes I think you don't give a damn about anyone but yourself. No, you can't see Kelly. You've done enough to destroy his life."

"That's kind of harsh. I didn't put a gun to his head, you know."

"If you love him, the kindest thing you can do is stay away. He made it clear in the hospital that it was over. He made his choice. Now help him keep it."

"Are you really mad at me, Mom?"

"Yep."

"Do you still love me?" asked Asa with trepidation.

"Silly goose. I'm just mad." I kissed her forehead. "You are my shining star . . . my shining star I'd like to kick in the tuckus right now."

"Did you never make mistakes when you were young?"

"When I was young! I make mistakes all the time still. It's the process of being human. It's because I am your mother that I can bitch about your mistakes. It's one of life's little pleasures."

"I see." Asa put down her teacup. "Well, I have a dinner date so I have to dress."

"I can see that I'm being dismissed. Okay, I'll go over to Kelly's house and try to see his wife, if she will let me in the door."

"You'll do fine, Mother," sighed Asa.

"I always do." Since I liked having the last word, I bounced happily to my car.

20

Asa watched her mother leave the hotel. Looking out a lobby window, Asa made sure Josiah got into her car safely and drove away.

She sincerely hoped that her mother could get Kelly's life back on track. Asa realized how selfish she had been with Kelly and felt sorry she had started the affair. Asa loved Kelly deeply and was now worried that she had ruined his life.

Exhausted, she climbed up the staircase to her room. Unlocking the door, she felt for the light switch before stepping into the room.

Someone grabbed her arm and pulled her into the room, placing his hand over her mouth before she could react. "Don't kick, Asa," a familiar voice whispered in her ear, "and I'll let you go."

Recognizing the voice, Asa slumped against the body holding her. She inhaled his cologne and masculine smell.

The aromas brought back intense memories that brought her both pleasure and pain.

"I'm going to take my hand down. Okay?"

Asa nodded.

"Don't turn on the light."

She could not bring herself to move away from him. Being in his arms felt like home, even though she knew he was the enemy. Damn. She could never trust herself with him.

He didn't pull away either, but took the occasion to deeply breathe in her shiny hair and warm luscious skin. "You always smell like Paris after a spring shower," he murmured as he clasped his hands around her waist.

"What are you doing here, Minor?" asked Asa, trying to find the resolve to push him away.

Minor's hands ran up and down her blouse.

Asa gasped with pleasure.

"You surprised me at my hotel room. I thought I'd return the favor." He nuzzled her neck.

Asa moaned.

Minor pulled Asa over to the bed and threw her down. Kicking her legs apart, he placed himself between them and leaning over, gave Asa a deep kiss.

She hated herself for kissing him back. She hated herself for wanting him . . . still, after his betrayal so many years ago. Minor was a sickness with her.

Kelly was her soul mate, a person she would love until her last breath, but her feelings for Minor were built on heat and need. Asa hadn't realized how much she had needed Minor to touch her through the years, but now she exploded with need and she didn't care what the consequences might be.

21

Mark Twain once said, "I want to be in Kentucky when the end of the world comes, because it's always twenty years behind."

I don't think Mr. Twain was wrong then and I don't think he's wrong now.

I was mulling this over as I drove around Cheapside, looking for a parking space. I circled the block around the old Courthouse several times, not finding a parking space. The old Courthouse used to be the site of the old slave market in Lexington. Passing, I saw two statues of Thomas Hunt Morgan and John C. Breckinridge glorifying the Confederate side of the Civil War.

Even though Kentucky was a border state and stayed in the Union, there are no statues honoring the glorious dead of boys in blue around the old Courthouse. There were also no statues to those Lexingtonians who changed the world for the positive. No carved stone to commemorate Lexington citizens like Morgan's nephew, Thomas Hunt Morgan, a Nobel Prize winner for his discovery of the role that chromosomes play in heredity.

Then there was Mary Breckinridge, John C. Breckinridge's granddaughter, who founded the Frontier Nursing Service, which serviced the health of women and children in Eastern Kentucky. Intrepid nurses rode on horses or mules into the mountains to visit families, as there were no paved roads. They even rode in the snow and rain into hollers with their nursing supplies in saddlebags.

Another notable was Harriet Van Meter, who founded the International Book Project. In 1966, Miss Harriet placed an ad in an English-speaking newspaper in India offering to send books to whoever needed them. She got responses and began sending books from her basement.

Today, IBP sends over 200,000 English-language books overseas annually.

Miss Harriet was nominated for a Nobel Peace Prize and was recognized as a "Partner For Peace" by President George H. W. Bush.

Where are their statues? They certainly did more to change the world for the better than their Confederate ancestors.

But I digress. You gotta love it when you think about the South hanging on to its past, but now for the fun part of our history. Since we are talking about statues, let's talk about Black Bess.

Black Bess was the famous mare belonging to John Hunt Morgan, the Thunderbolt of the Confederacy. She was one of the more famous horses of the Civil War. One could say she was a veteran of the War, but even though she carried John Hunt Morgan through many a skirmish, she was not deemed heroic enough for the statue at the old Courthouse (even female animals get cheated out of their place in history), so the sculptor, Pompeo Coppini, made the horse a stallion.

Of course, horse lovers took offense and for many years, frat boys took it upon themselves to paint the horse's, umm, testicles in protest.

> So darkness comes to Bluegrass men
> Like darkness o'er them falls
> For well we know gentlemen should show
> Respect for a lady's balls.

Because I was thinking about all of this, I missed a parking space and had to go around the square again. Giving up parking on the street, I settled on a parking lot, grabbed my ticket, and handed over my car keys to the attendant. This was something I was loath to do, as it provided a way for some unscrupulous person to copy my keys, but I also had to gauge how far I had to walk.

Comfort over paranoia.

I limped my way to Shaneika's office. Feeling rather righteous, I poo-poo'd the secretary when she asked me if I had an appointment and brushed past her into Shaneika's office.

Shaneika looked up from some briefs when I opened the door. "Don't you even bother to knock?" She waved her secretary away. "I could have had a client in here."

"All will be forgiven when I tell you the news," I replied confidently. I looked about her office, taking in all the relics and heirlooms of the Civil War–a Confederate officer's sword, a framed fragment of a Confederate battle flag, a letter from Lincoln to his wife's brother, a photograph of African-American women washing clothes at Camp Nelson, a small painting of Generals Lee and Grant at Appomattox, a silver Mint Julep cup from the Todd family, and so forth. Her office was a shrine, and no matter how many times I asked, Shaneika would not discuss the artifacts, except to say they were family heirlooms.

I wanted juicy details.

"What's your news?"

"There's no corpse."

Shaneika sat silent for a moment and then asked, "No corpse as in 'can't find it yet' or 'there was never a person inside the gondola?'"

"As in, there is no body and will never be as Charlie was not in the gondola."

"Hmm. Isn't that interesting? Why do you think the ATF was chewing up my panties then?"

"I think it was part of a ruse to get back at Asa."

"I wish they'd get over her. I guess the harassment will go on until everyone connected with Asa's story dies or retires."

We sat in silence with our collective thoughts until Shaneika asked, "How do you know that Charlie wasn't in the gondola?"

I suddenly found my feet very interesting.

"Josiah, have you been peeking in keyholes again?"

"Kinda. Can't tell you so you have deniability if asked."

"So you were not told officially?"

I shook my head.

"Nice talking with you, Josiah." Shaneika went back to her brief.

But I knew Shaneika wasn't angry because she was wearing a smile. Barely visible, but it was there.

22

Asa unlocked the door to the Butterfly and disarmed the alarm system. Hearing a growl, Asa quickly whirled around and said, "Baby, it's me," before the two-hundred twenty-five pound Mastiff could knock her to the floor and sit on her.

Reassured, Baby bounded over to Asa, sniffed while drooling on her pants, and then happily stuck his snout in her crotch waiting for his ears to be scratched.

Asa bent down and kissed the scar on Baby's forehead. "Baby, is it possible that you are getting prettier each time I see you? Yes, you are. Yes, you are. You are so pretty and strong. I love you, Baby. Yes, I do."

Baby looked happily up at Asa and then sneezed all over her before licking the slobber off her hands.

"I love everything about you, but the fluids," laughed Asa, going into the kitchen for towels. "I don't know how Mother keeps this house clean with you salivating over everything."

Baby padded after her, but refused to let Asa clean his face.

Giving up, Asa threw the towel on the kitchen counter. "Let's find Kelly, shall we? Do you know where Kelly is? Go find him for me."

Asa followed Baby as he led her to one of the guest bedrooms. Knocking on the door, she listened but heard no answer. Quietly opening the door, she entered and found Kelly spread out, asleep on the bed. An empty bottle of vodka sat on the floor.

Asa let out a long sigh. *This is my fault*, she thought as she covered Kelly with a blanket. Baby took up residence next to the bed while Asa settled in a chair. It wasn't long before several cats of the Kitty Kaboodle Gang joined them.

One crawled into Asa's lap and fell asleep.

But Asa didn't sleep. She watched Kelly take one deep breath after another as she pondered what to do.

Asa decided that she would tell Kelly the truth for once. The truth would be hard to utter because it was so ugly–so very ugly, because it was so selfish.

23

A huge wet nose bounced on the bed.

Kelly opened one eye after inhaling hot moist doggy breath.

Directly in front of him bobbed a large droopy furry face with a huge tongue dripping slime. One dark friendly eye blinked while the other eye, ruined and scarred from a gunshot, sat motionless in its socket. The entire head shook with excitement when Kelly sat up in recognition.

"Hello Baby," moaned Kelly. He then opened his other eye.

Behind Baby, Asa came into focus, staring back at him.

Kelly shook his head and looked again.

Asa was still staring at him.

"What are you doing here?" sneered Kelly, realizing that he was not hallucinating.

"Mother told me that you were sleeping one off at her house. I see that you got into her stash of vodka."

"So what? What do you care?" Kelly tried to wipe the taste of vomit and vodka from his mouth.

"I care very much."

"You don't care about anyone but yourself and never have."

Asa flinched, but her expression remained neutral. "I'm here to set things right between us."

"Too little, too late."

"Shut up and listen."

"Go screw yourself, Asa."

Asa reached over and slapped Kelly's face.

Kelly gasped in surprise as his hand flew to his face and gingerly touched where she had struck him.

"I'm here because you are messing up your life. You think your misery is due to the fact that I don't love you, but you're wrong. Besides my mother, you are the person I love most in the world. You are the first person I think about when I awake each morning and the last person when I go to bed. It has been that way since I was fourteen."

Kelly snarled, "Why did you leave after high school without even saying goodbye? Have you any idea what that did to me? How it shattered me?"

"It broke me too, but it had to be done."

"Why, Asa? Why bring such unhappiness to us both? I couldn't believe it when I found out that you married that Minor Reasor creep and not me. It crushed my heart. It destroyed me."

"Believe me when I say that I have always loved you, but I knew I could never be what you wanted me to be.

"You wanted a wife and children. You wanted fried chicken dinners on lazy summer afternoons, a four bedroom house by a running stream, and a riding mower to mow the yard. You wanted a normal family life.

"I could never have given you that. There is a darkness in me that I don't understand. How could I expect you to? I loved you enough to give you up so that you could have the things you wanted and needed."

Kelly was unfazed in his bitterness. "We could have worked things out."

Asa shook her head. "We would have gotten married, but in the end I would have left."

"No, we would have worked it out."

"Do you love your wife?"

"Yes." Kelly nodded.

"Do you love your children?"

"Of course."

"Were you happy?"

"I was content," confessed Kelly.

"You would never have been with me. I was a bird that would have wanted to fly away every day. Our life together would have been too small for me.

"Know that I love you with all my heart and I gave you up so that you could live the life you wanted. Rejoice in the time we had together. It was precious, but we couldn't build a future on it."

"I love you too, Asa," said Kelly, his eyes filling with tears. "I have never loved anyone as I have loved you."

"You made the right choice when you left me at the hospital. Build a life with your wife and children. Celebrate what we once had and still feel for each other. I will love you until my dying breath, but I am not right for you, my beloved."

"Why did you marry Minor?"

Asa thought for a moment. "I was young. I was lonely. I thought he would protect me, and then when I found out he was the enemy, it was too late." Asa reached over and clasped Kelly's trembling hand. "It was never like that with us. Never. Oh, my darling. Please go back to your life and be happy for the both of us. I can only continue if I know that you are safe and well. No tears. No tears. We had our time together."

Kelly kissed Asa's hand and rubbed it against his rough, unshaven face. "Asa. Asa."

Asa wrapped her arms around Kelly. They held each other in silence, and finally at peace.

24

How did Charlie Hoskins get out of the balloon's gondola?

Witnesses saw him get into the gondola at Bowman Field and watched the balloon rise. So how did he get out?

I pulled out a map of Louisville and found where Bowman Field and Churchill Downs were located.

Bowman Field was east of Churchill Downs. Directly between them were Seneca Gardens, Calvary Cemetery, and Audubon Park, all three green spaces where a large hot air balloon could settle down. However, Seneca Gardens and Audubon Park were heavily used. A hot air balloon landing in those places would have been seen, and so far no one has stepped forward to say that they had seen a balloon land in either park.

A cemetery would have fewer witnesses, at least the kind that stand upright and talk, but also less green space to set down a balloon. There was a possibility that Charlie had landed the balloon on a building and jumped out.

Still, how did he guide the balloon to Churchill Downs?

I knew my daughter would know how he could have landed it, but I didn't want to involve her any further in this mess. I really wanted Asa to leave, but she kept hanging around.

Was it because Minor was still in town?

I pushed that thought from my mind. Putting Asa near Minor was like throwing gasoline on an oil fire. Those two burned with something unholy and it made me fear for Asa.

However, I did have another name in my hamper of know-it-alls.

I dialed a number on my old rotary phone. An answering machine picked up.

"I know you're back. I need you. Your mission, should you decide to accept, is to help Shaneika. As always, should either one of us be caught or killed, the secretary will disavow any knowledge of our actions. This tape will self-destruct in five seconds."

I heard the phone click on.

"What the hell do you want now?"

"Helllllloooo, Franklin."

25

"Can't this toy car go a little faster?"

Franklin patted his steering wheel. "Don't listen to the bad lady, Sweetie. You're doing fine."

I tried to get comfortable, but who could in a tiny Smart Car? I had to yell to be heard because the engine was so loud. "We should have taken my car. We're never going to get to Louisville at this speed." Spying a car rental business, I grabbed the steering wheel and jerked it, sending the car screeching into the parking lot.

It took a long time for Franklin to quit screaming. "You could have gotten us killed," he yelled.

But I didn't hear his complaints as I was already out, heading toward the office. A few minutes later, I emerged from the office as a silver Mercedes SUV pulled to a stop in front of me. After signing some papers, I threw the keys to Franklin.

Franklin reluctantly got in. "I just wanted my baby to stretch her legs a bit."

"Consider them stretched. We'll catch her on the way back."

Franklin threw a kiss at his Smart Car and then pulled out onto Versailles Road after spending a long time making his motorized seat go forward, backward, up, then down, forward again, and back up until he got it just right.

"Come on. Put the pedal to the metal."

"I don't see why I needed to come on this fruitless adventure of yours."

"Do shut up with that complaining. You know I can't drive long distances. Besides, you know about hot air ballooning."

Franklin smirked. "I know a little. My uncle was heavy into it when I was a teenager, but it got too expensive so he had to give it up."

"A little is more than I know." I confided in Franklin about Charlie Hoskins' balloon exploding over Churchill Downs, but that he wasn't found in the wreckage.

"That's ridiculous."

"How so?"

"The idea that Charlie Hoskins could have taken off at Bowman Field and then precisely landed at Churchill Downs is ludicrous."

"Why?"

"Because there is no steering mechanism in hot air balloons. They drift with the wind."

"You can't steer them at all?"

"Only somewhat. You can change altitudes. That will change the direction of the balloon."

"Well?"

"But you can't make the wind go in the direction you want even if you change altitudes. That is very unpredictable at best, even if you send a test balloon out first."

"Is that done?"

"Yes, but you are still talking about great odds. And during the most important race day of the year? My goodness. Churchill Downs, racehorse owners, and spectators would have sued Charlie. He would have been arrested. His pilot's license might have been revoked. It would have been a mess. No amount of publicity would have been worth the chaos he would have to face."

"It was a mess with the explosion." I thought for a moment. "Maybe it was a con."

"A con?"

"Since Charlie wasn't found, maybe the whole balloon thing was a red herring."

"A red herring?"

"Would you please quit repeating me?"

"You want me to quit repeating you?"

Ignoring Franklin, I continued, "His body wasn't found as Charlie was not in the gondola."

"But you said there were plenty of witnesses who saw him get into it."

"How can a person get out of a balloon after it's been released?"

Franklin yapped while zipping past cars in the left lane. "Every balloon is equipped with drop lines that can be thrown out for the ground crew to use to guide the balloon in landing."

"Could someone use a drop line to climb out of a gondola if they were close to the ground?"

"Again, it would be very dangerous, but I guess it could be done."

"What about a parachute?"

"Wouldn't work. Hot air balloons don't get high enough for a parachute to work."

"What about a bungee cord?"

Franklin shrugged. "I don't see an older man using a bungee cord and diving out of a hot air balloon. Besides, people would have seen."

"Would they? That Saturday, people in Louisville were either at Churchill Downs or at Derby parties. Derby Day is the most iconic day in Louisville. Very few people would be out and about."

"Perhaps you're right," Franklin concurred as he pulled into Bowman Field.

I went into the office and made up some story about doing a travel blog on hot air ballooning and how I wanted to talk with Charlie Hoskins' crew since the explosion was so relevant to my story. I swear my nose grew an inch or so.

The secretary in the office chatted about how she wanted to write her own blog and asked questions about getting started. My nose grew another inch responding, but at the end of my suggestions, the happy secretary pointed to a man tinkering with a small airplane near the office.

As I went over to the man in overalls, I waved to Franklin to join us since he would know what questions to ask.

I introduced myself and then Franklin as my assistant. The man, John Turner, turned out to be Charlie's ground crew headman and he was as bewildered as everyone else. At first he refused to talk with us, but Franklin flashed a hundred dollar bill and promised that everything he said would be off the record.

"I have talked to every outfit there is—FBI, ATF, FAA, State Police, local police, and some other agencies I've never heard of. I haven't a clue as to what happened except that Charlie never showed up."

"What do you mean?" I asked. "He got in the basket and flew away. Charlie was seen by lots of people."

John shook his head. "That's the problem. We were not supposed to take off from here. Charlie had a new balloon made with a picture of Persian Blue and Charlie's name on it to use that day. I had rented a parking lot in the industrial part of town on the west side. We had set it up, ready to go that morning, but Charlie never showed up.

"I called his cell phone, his office, his assistant, his wife. I even started calling hospitals. No one had seen him and everyone assumed he was with me."

"And he wasn't?" I questioned again.

John shook his head.

"Was Charlie to navigate the balloon?" asked Franklin.

John replied, "No, we had an experienced pilot for that. We had made arrangements with the network televising the race that the balloon was supposed to drift near Churchill Downs, they would get a shot, and then we would bring the balloon down. It was a publicity stunt, that's all."

"So the balloon was never to fly over Churchill Downs?" I asked.

"Good gawd, are you crazy?" sputtered John. "That would have landed us in jail, not to mention everyone on the crew would have lost their license. We would have been banned from every airport in the country except as passengers."

"I'm very confused," I remarked.

"You and me both," confessed John.

Franklin gave us both one of his smug looks. "I think I've got it."

"Enlighten us," I suggested.

"Charlie comes up with this publicity stunt and has a new balloon made. I would say it cost a pretty penny—anywhere from fifty to seventy-five thousand. Right?"

John nodded. "Sixty is about right."

Franklin smiled and continued, "He tells his regular crew that he has arranged a publicity stunt with the network for Derby morning. He gets you to make arrangements to rent out a suitable area to stage the ascent of the balloon."

"So far so good," replied John.

"Since you hired a pilot, I assume Charlie was going to arrive only to check on the balloon and then head over to Churchill Downs where a reporter would be waiting to interview him when the balloon came into view."

John looked at me and then at Franklin. "You make it sound so simple. Yeah. Yeah. That's exactly what was to happen."

"But Charlie never arrived to give the go ahead, so you did not release the balloon," I said.

"Finally, someone who gets it," declared John, the lines of stress on his face suddenly disappearing.

Franklin continued, "So Charlie doesn't arrive, you don't release the new balloon, and then you look up and see Charlie's old balloon in the sky."

"I about messed in my drawers," confessed John. "Sorry, ma'am."

"So what happened then?" I asked.

"I called Bowman Field and the manager tells me that Charlie set up his old balloon there and lifted off in it." John looked distressed again. "It was suicide. A very dangerous flight plan. To get to Churchill Downs, he would have to go over the expressway, and depending on the air currents, he could possibly drift too close to the airport. Nobody in his right mind would have chosen that way."

Franklin pursed his lips. "And yet he made it to Churchill Downs."

John shrugged. "I don't know how Charlie managed it."

"Then the balloon exploded," Franklin uttered.

"Yeah, it went down in flames. We could see most of the explosion from where we were. I'm not ashamed to tell you that I prayed and I'm not a praying man. I'm just so glad that no one else was hurt."

I looked askance at John. "So you think Charlie is dead?"

"Of course. If he was in that gondola, he died instantly, I hope. I'm going to his memorial this Saturday."

"Which is where?" I asked.

While John was busy giving the details of Charlie's memorial, Franklin went into the office. By the time he came out, I was already waiting in the Mercedes and was nodding off.

"What did you find out?" I asked.

Franklin gave me that smug look again. "I know the how, but I don't know the why. That's your department."

"How can there be a memorial when there is no Charlie?"

"Apparently Charlie left instructions with his lawyer about what to do if and when he passed on. Everyone thinks he's dead, so the lawyer is having Charlie's memorial."

"How convenient," I muttered. "Are you going to spill on the how?"

"Maybe during lunch, which you are going to buy and then only if you spill why you are so interested. Charlie Hoskins was nothing to you," stated Franklin, revving up the car.

"That's easy. I will be happy to buy you lunch and I can tell you why right now. It's because Minor Reasor is on this case."

"And who is Minor Reasor?"

"Asa's ex-husband!"

"Get out!" exclaimed Franklin, slapping me on the arm. "This is getting better and better. You are going to tell me everything, and I mean everything, Josiah."

I didn't resist. I was tired of secrets. I was tired of tiptoeing over Asa's past.

For some reason Asa was staying in town.

Was it to help Kelly?

Was it to help Shaneika?

Was it to exact revenge on Minor?

Was it to start up with Minor again?

For once I wanted Asa to leave town. I feared whatever she was up to was going to blow up in all our faces.

And what about Goetz? What was he doing talking to Minor–an ATF agent? What connection did those two have? They talked as if they were old acquaintances.

I needed to talk to someone who wasn't involved, who could help me see through all the smokescreens. I was too rattled by Minor being in town to think straight.

Franklin had a keen mind. If anybody could untangle this massive web, he might be the one.

26

We stopped to grab something to eat. As soon as Franklin picked up his turkey sandwich, he gushed, "I want to hear all of the misery. Don't leave anything out."

"Don't gloat so, Franklin. It's unseemly."

"Spill it all, or my lips are sealed about what I've learned."

"You know that you're a pain."

"Is that the pot calling the kettle black? Let's not squabble." Franklin reached over and pinched my arm. "Give!"

"Geez, what a little monster." I rubbed my arm. "Let me get my thoughts straight."

Franklin twisted his mouth in agitation. "Come on. You're stalling."

"I have to start at the beginning. The very beginning of my downfall, and Asa's too."

"I'm listening," cooed Franklin gleefully.

"For years, Brannon and I flew high. Our careers were going in the right direction—up. Brannon was making lots of money with his architectural firm and together we bought some land and developed it. That's where we made our big money.

"Along the way, Brannon refurbished Lady Elsmere's house and through her, we knew everyone in town. We were invited to all the best parties, and I was on all the important boards in town. We were happy, or so I thought.

"I think things started slipping when Asa left home right after high school. She didn't say goodbye to Kelly and I think that bit of selfishness created a crack that got bigger and bigger as time went on until it was a chasm that we all fell into."

"You blame Asa?"

"No, I don't blame her, but I think one action creates a reaction, which creates another reaction until it snowballs." I shook my head, brandishing a potato chip. "Or maybe each person is allotted only a specific time for happiness and when it's up, it's up."

"So what happened?" asked Franklin before biting into his sandwich.

"We didn't hear from Asa all summer. I was worried sick. Then we got a call from her that she was in college and to send tuition money, which we did. After that, contact was sporadic. She never came home for the summers, although she would send her transcripts. Asa's marks were very high, so she wasn't fooling around at school, but then other cracks started to appear."

Franklin leaned forward. "Yes?"

"You are so ghoulish, delighting in my ruin. Really, Franklin, have you no compassion?"

"Compassion is overrated. Get on with the story."

"I was next in line for the job of Dean over the Art Department when he retired. One afternoon he called me into his office, and said that due to extenuating circumstances, the job was going to be offered to another colleague.

"You can imagine I was stunned. After all, I had all the credentials and seniority in the department to be in line for his job."

"What did you do?"

"Nothing. I had no idea why and the Dean wouldn't enlighten me. I went back to my office, had a good cry, and then went about my duties. I wasn't the first person to be passed over for a job, and I wouldn't be the last, but it really bothered me." I sat in silence, looking out the window, remembering.

"And?"

"I started hearing whispering and giggling in the hallways for weeks, and more than once I distinctly heard Brannon's name. I began to put the pieces together. Since Asa's abrupt departure, Brannon seemed discontented and was often absent from home for long periods of time."

"Did you ask him about it?"

"At first. But he would get very angry, and we would end up in a huge fight."

"No defense like a good offense."

"Precisely, but I got sidelined. By that time, Asa had graduated and was working for the Secret Service. I got a call from her one night that she was going to blow the whistle to the Washington Post about some serious irregularities within her department."

"This is where I have some common knowledge."

"So does everyone. But it wasn't supposed to be like that. Her identity was supposed to be kept a secret, but someone leaked Asa's name as the informer."

"That's how I knew who Asa was. Her face was splashed everywhere and she even made the cover of *People*."

I continued, "Asa uncovered corruption within the Secret Service. She discovered that agents were having prostitutes in their hotel rooms and doing blow when they were on duty protecting important political figures. People's safety was seriously compromised."

"Why didn't Asa go to the Director?"

"She did and was told to keep her mouth shut. That's when she decided to go to the press."

"And then the word got out who had spilled the beans."

I nodded. "After that, Asa was subpoenaed to testify before several televised Congressional Committee hearings. Based on her testimony, her boss and several agents were fired. The entire agency was turned upside down."

Frank picked up the story. "Asa becomes an overnight sensation during the hearings due to her looks and testimony. The media really played her up as some sort of savior for the agency. Then drugs were found in Asa's car. If I remember correctly, the police said someone called in a tip."

I nodded. "Yes, and due to the amount of drugs found, she was charged with a felony. That's when all hell broke loose. Someone was out to discredit Asa and ruin her life."

Franklin had finished his sandwich and leaned back in his chair. "You think her husband planted those drugs in her car?"

I spat out the words, "Asa had only been married to Minor for less than a year. Minor was a company man all the way and did not agree with Asa blowing the whistle.

"As soon as Asa was arrested, he deserted her. She did not see him again until he testified against her at the trial."

"I remember watching it."

"Yeah, wasn't that great. Since Asa now had a huge profile with the public, the judge let the trial be televised. What a kangaroo court."

"But the beautiful Asa does not get convicted."

"Only because her fingerprints were not on the drugs. They were so stupid they didn't even think of that."

"Who are they?"

"The people she told on, the buddies of the fired guys, anyone with a grudge against women working in that field. Take your pick."

"I know what happened after that," interrupted Franklin.

"You mortgage the Butterfly up to the hilt to pay for Asa's legal fees, you quit your job due to all the snickering and politics at work, start raising honeybees. Brannon keeps it a secret that he sold his share of his business and hides the money only to leave you for a woman young enough to be his daughter. Asa recoups and starts her own security firm while you refuse to divorce Brannon if he doesn't cough up some dough. Meanwhile, you meet Matt, ergo me. Then Brannon has the bad taste to die of a heart attack, leaving you with no idea where all the money is, but you suspect the child mistress does. Last but not least, Richard Pidgeon dies in one of your hives, which causes an old grudge to surface in the form of the one and only Fred O'nan, who shoots Baby, me, and then eventually Matt in that order, and throws you over a cliff. Does that sum it up?"

"Pretty much. What a soap opera," I concurred.

"All we need is some beer to cry into."

I laughed. "I don't mean to be dramatic, but the last five years have been a bitch, to say the least."

Franklin laughed too. "At least you can say it hasn't been boring." He lifted his glass in salute. "But lady, you are still here to tell the tale," boasted Franklin, tapping the table, "and so am I."

I clicked my glass with his. "To bitches everywhere, long may we reign!"

27

"I have recounted my tale of woe," I reminded him. "Now give up what you know."

"The entire thing was a set-up."

"What do you mean, Franklin?"

"I went back into the office and pumped one of the security guards. Always talk to the people low on the totem pole. The big shots will hide things to cover their fannies, but the poorly paid will always cough up the truth, especially when they see a Ulysses S. Grant."

"What did he say?"

"*She* said that Charlie came with a new crew to help him get his balloon in position."

"So she had never seen them before?"

"Correctamundo! And she said the gondola had been modified."

"In what way?"

"There were tubes on the underside of the gondola and Charlie was very anxious about them."

"Anxious how?"

"He was yelling at the new crew not to damage them."

"Did she know what they were?"

"She thought they looked like some sort of a propellant."

"Did anyone in the office know of the flight plan?"

"According to the lovely lady in the hideous security uniform, the balloon was to head north toward the river. It was never to approach Churchill Downs," reported Franklin.

I thought for a moment. "None of this makes any sense. I don't understand it at all."

Franklin looked smug. "I think I do."

"Okay, give."

"Everything was a ruse. Charlie needed to get his experienced crew out of the way, so he sent them on a wild goose chase to the west side of town on the pretext of getting his new balloon ready for a flight."

"But Charlie never intended for that balloon to fly that day," I added.

"That's correct."

"That's one piece of the puzzle. What's the rest?" I asked.

"I think it's safe to say that Charlie had his usual balloon modified. He never intended to fly north. That was another lie. I think his real intention was to fly the balloon to Churchill Downs all along."

"But why?"

"To have it explode."

"Why not have it explode over the Ohio River?"

"Because there were certain people at Churchill Downs that needed to witness the balloon explode firsthand."

I must have looked confused as Franklin moved our plates aside and positioned the salt and pepper shakers. "The pepper shaker is the red herring."

"The new balloon?"

"Yes, it was made to keep his real crew away from the modified balloon." He held up the salt shaker. "This is the modified balloon. Charlie lied about his flight plan because he didn't want to be tracked. He brings a new crew and takes off."

"Then what?"

"Somewhere along the line, Charlie gets out of the balloon. Remember all that green space between Bowman Field and the expressway? Somewhere in there his new crew helps him out of the basket and whisks him away."

"How does he get out of the gondola?"

"If he lowers the balloon enough, he can climb down the rope to the ground or the top of a building, just like we surmised. Or maybe they installed an air cushion like stuntmen use when they fall off buildings. Charlie lowers the balloon enough to jump out. The air cushion catches him and off he goes. The crew let the air out and poof, it's gone in a truck.

"The new crew follows with a car in which Charlie makes his getaway. Then the balloon is made to go toward Churchill Downs by remote control."

"What causes the explosion?"

"A planted pipe bomb that goes off by remote."

"Still, Franklin, why would Charlie do such a thing when he had a horse running in the Kentucky Derby? Most people would give their eye teeth to be in his position."

"I don't know the why, but Charlie needed to stage his death and he did so very cleverly. My guess is to follow the money. Gambling debts? Wanted to leave his wife? Something was not on the up and up with Persian Blue perhaps? Get your new stud muffin to do some snooping for you."

I frowned. "I don't know if I'll continue seeing Goetz."

Franklin feigned astonishment. "Trouble in paradise? I like to know that I'm not the only one without a prom date this spring."

I pursed my lips.

"What? No catchy reply. What did Mr. No Nonsense do?" Franklin batted his eyes.

"I caught him in a lie."

Franklin reared back in his chair. "Is that all? You lie all the time."

"I most certainly do not," I argued. After thinking for a moment, I retracted my statement. "If I do lie, it's because I either don't want to hurt someone's feelings or

I'm in pursuit of information. Sometimes you have to fudge a little here and there to find out the greater truth."

"Is that how you justify it?"

"We are talking about Charlie, not me."

"No. You started talking about Detective Goetz, whom you are thinking of shelving for telling a fib."

"This was something more serious. Deception on a grand scale. I caught him having a secret rendezvous with Minor."

Franklin's eyes widened. "Really? That does go from modest fibbing to fetching the knife out of the drawer to stab you in the back."

"That's a reassuring thing to say."

Franklin grabbed the tab and reached for his wallet.

"I thought I was to get this," I said.

"Thought I'd pay for your last meal."

"Very cute." Quick with the witty repartees, aren't I?

"You're seeing a man who was partner to a cop that tried to kill you several times and now you find out that he is having a secret tryst with Asa's evil husband at his apartment. I would say that you are playing with fire there."

Franklin threw some bills on the table and waved to the waitress. "And knowing you, this will be handled like a bull in a china shop."

"What would you do?"

"Pack my bags and leave town."

"I can't do that with Asa involved somehow. I feel that Minor is trying to drag her into a new mess."

"Pack her bag as well and leave town together."

"What are you going to do, Franklin?"

"I am taking my own advice–leaving town."

"Coward," I accused.

"Just follow the money. This is not about sex or power. It's about the green stuff that makes the world go round."

"Why money?"

"Remember what the guy looks like? No woman would go gaga over him unless she was blind and stupid. As for power, he's a two-bit developer with grand notions. If he wanted to puff himself up a bit here and there, no one cared because no one really took Charlie seriously.

"Whatever went down with Charlie Hoskins went down because of that horse. I'll bet you a hundred to one."

"Where shall I send your winnings?" I asked.

"To California. I'm going to see Matt. At least in California, the nuts are friendly."

I really couldn't blame him. The temptation to leave town was overwhelming.

Maybe I could talk Asa into joining me in Europe. I was just tired of all the drama.

A few days at the British Museum would set me straight.

28

"Is something wrong with your meal?" asked Goetz.

"No, it's fine," I replied.

"You're just picking at it."

"I guess I'm not very hungry."

"When have you ever turned down a free meal?"

I made a face. "I think I've cooked a lot of free meals for you."

Goetz put down his fork. "Geez, don't be so touchy. I was just kidding." He leaned back in his chair and scrutinized me. "What's going on?"

"Nothing. Look, I'm eating." I took a bite of my lobster salad.

"You seem off tonight. Everything okay? You're not out of money again, are you?"

"I harvested Locust honey this week and the Butterfly is raking in money from the receptions that Eunice is booking. Frankly, I'd be on welfare if it wasn't for that woman taking over my finances."

"That's an odd thing to say. When have you ever given up control of anything in your life?"

"Maybe I'm tired of being what I'm not. I used to think I was hot stuff, one of the go-getters in this town, but I'm just a broken-down old has-been."

"Oh, Lordy, let's get out the violins. What happened to make you throw in the towel?"

I shrugged.

"I have never seen you so down and out."

"Maybe something happened to make me lose my faith in my fellow man. Maybe someone close to me is a deceiver."

"I told you Franklin would stab you in the back sooner or later. I never liked that guy."

"You don't like Franklin because he's gay. He threatens you, but he's not the one."

"Why are you looking at me?"

"Really? You want to play this game?"

"I don't know what you're talking about," answered Goetz, raising his voice a little.

"What was Minor Reasor doing in your apartment?"

Goetz looked at me, stunned.

"Well?"

"Holy crap! You *were* listening at the door. I should have known—a busybody like you." Goetz waved at the waitress and threw a large bill down on the table. "We're done here," he said as he grabbed my arm, pulling me out of the restaurant.

"You're hurting me!" I complained.

"Shut up, Josiah. For once in your life, take some advice and keep your trap shut."

"I can't walk this fast. You're hurting my bad leg."

"I'm gonna wring your neck if you don't get in the car."

I glanced at Goetz' face as he tugged me along. It was angry. Really angry.

I felt fear. The same kind of fear I'd felt with Fred O'nan.

Was Goetz going to hurt me?

I started pulling away when Goetz swept me up with one arm and unlocked the car door with the other. I couldn't get away. His arm was like iron.

He pushed me into the car. "Now sit there and be quiet."

While he went around to the other side of the car, I fumbled for my purse in the back seat and searched for my stun gun.

When Goetz got in the car, I brandished my stun gun and said, "Don't you touch me again. I'm getting a cab home."

Goetz grabbed my wrist and simply took the stun gun out of my hand. He threw it in the back seat. "Buckle up," was all he said.

He drove out of the parking lot and onto the main artery, not stopping until we arrived at Goetz' favorite burger joint.

Goetz pulled up to the outdoor speaker and lowered his window. "Hi. We'll have six cheeseburgers, two large fries, and a sweet tea." He looked at me. "Do you want a frosty malt?"

I nodded.

"And a frosty malt. Make sure there's lots of ketchup. Thanks."

He drove to the pay window and collected our food. From there we drove to a park where we ate in silence for the most part.

While sucking on my frosty malt, I remarked, "Well, it looks like you're not going to kill me, so what's the plan?"

"What I'm going to tell you is all confidential–strictly off the record. No blabbing to Asa or Shaneika."

I hesitated. "I don't know."

"Then I'm not going to tell you a thing."

"I promise."

"Promise what? Sometimes dealing with you is like dealing with a kid."

"I promise not to tell anyone what you are about to tell me in confidence–cross my heart and hope to die."

Satisfied, Goetz settled back in his seat. "Minor and I go way back. I was an informer for the ATF and I reported to him."

"Did your boss know about you?"

"No, that's the point of being an informer–no one outside the loop knows."

"What would you tell Minor?"

"All law enforcement agencies are territorial. They don't like to share information. I would tell Minor about things I heard."

"Like what?"

"Like a rumor that a sheriff in another county was taking bribes to look the other way on smuggling or money laundering through car dealerships or little country stores. Things like that."

"Why did you do it?"

"I needed the money."

"You got paid?"

"Of course. I was taking big risks. I wanted money for my trouble."

"Asa has never mentioned that she knew you."

"She didn't. Minor would never have told her about me."

"I still don't understand. Minor was stationed in Washington, not here."

"When I first started, he was in Kentucky. Once he was transferred to Washington, I told him that it was too risky to report to anyone else. I still report to Minor who passes the info on to agents who work this area. They didn't know who I am. It keeps me safe."

"You once told me that you knew Brannon. Was it because of Minor?"

"When Minor married Asa, I checked her out. I did a deep background check on you as well as Brannon."

I felt a shiver go up my spine. Who was this man sitting next to me, munching so casually on French fries? "What did you find out about my family?"

"Asa was the real deal. She bled red, white, and blue. You were respectable–maybe a little too eccentric for this town."

"What about Brannon? You said you didn't like him."

"You remember that?"

"Yeah."

"He was condescending to his staff, rude to his students, and just a plain ass to everyone else. I know for a fact that his partners were glad to see the back of him."

I was stunned. Was he describing the charming, intelligent man that I had known as my husband? Was he describing the real Brannon?

"You look like you don't believe me. You were the only thing that gave Brannon class. He never would have made it big without you. Trust me on this."

"You're not describing the man I knew as my husband."

"Oh yeah? Look how he treated you when he didn't want you anymore."

Tears flooded my eyes. "Stop it!"

"You know I'm telling the truth. You just don't want to admit that you picked the wrong man–that your marriage was a fraud. Brannon was a user and he used you."

"Are you using me?"

Goetz handed me some paper napkins. "I'm trying to steer you away from danger."

I dried my eyes. "I don't think we should see each other anymore. I don't feel that I can trust you. Everything is topsy-turvy."

Goetz grabbed my hand in his big paw. "Don't leave, Josiah. I need something shiny in my life. Too many things have been tarnished for me."

I shook my head. "I think we need to take a break. I need to wrap my head around this."

"Would you trust me if I told you something that you could hold over me?"

"What would that be?" I scoffed.

"I killed O'nan for you."

29

What do you say when a person confesses that he killed for you?

Gee, thanks for telling me and making me an accessory after the fact.
Thank you for saving my life and the life of my friend.
What do you want?
Are you going to kill me now that I know?
Stay away!

All of the above ran through my mind, but I said nothing.

Goetz took me home.

I belted back a few drinks and went to bed. The next morning I did what I always do when feeling discombobulated—I went to see my honeybees.

I sat in my golf cart, watching them fly in and out of their hives, buzzing to the spring flowers in the pastures.

When European settlers first came to Kentucky, they were surprised to find European honeybees making nests in trees. This was unusual as Apis mellifera was not native to the New World.

Native Americans called the bees, "flies with the fiery tails."

It turned out that the honeybees in Kentucky were descendants of the first honeybees brought to Virginia by European settlers, having expanded their territory by swarming.

The establishment of honeybees in an area was a warning to Native Americans that Europeans were not far behind.

Unfortunately for me, there had been no warning. I never had considered that Goetz had killed O'nan. I had always thought that Asa had one of her minions do the deed. But thinking about it, it made perfect sense.

Goetz told me how O'nan had threatened his grandchildren if he didn't help take me down. Believing his family was in danger, Goetz killed O'nan with a sniper shot, using me as bait.

It wasn't that I didn't want O'nan dead. I never believed I was capable of hating someone as much as I hated Fred O'nan.

But if O'nan really threatened Goetz' family, why didn't Goetz have him arrested?

Did he think another judge might be as lenient with O'nan as the first judge had been?

Did Goetz worry that O'nan might hire someone to act for him as he rotted in jail?

It seemed like a piece of the story was missing.

And why did I feel so conflicted?

Was it because Goetz had the guts to do what I should have done, but didn't because I lacked the courage?

And do I tell Matt? Oh, poor Matt. He got caught in the crossfire.

I felt so bad about that.

I sat for an hour or so, watching the bees fly past me, some lighting on me so they could scrape the pollen off their bodies into the pollen baskets on the back of their legs. If they landed on my arms, I'd coaxed them onto my hands so I could check them for mites or misshapen wings.

Bees can be handled. Like anything, you have to know how.

And like anything, you have to pick your battles carefully. Sometimes bees don't want to play. Sometimes it's dangerous to go near them.

I think that was the same with Goetz. I didn't think he was going to harm me. At least, not for a while.

Shaneika had called in the morning. It seems like the ATF were bent on making her life miserable. They had a search warrant for her office and home.

She wanted me to pick Linc up at school and bring him to the Butterfly where his grandmother, Eunice, and he would stay until Shaneika could clean up the mess the ATF left.

My path was clear. I needed to do more snooping.

30

I stopped off at the Big House with Linc in tow. Going through the kitchen, I left Linc happily ensconced at a table with Charles, who set a roast beef sandwich and a big piece of chess pie in front of him. As I left the room, Charles told me that I could find Lady Elsmere having tea in the library.

I knocked on the library door and then opened it to find Liam also having tea with her Ladyship.

Upon seeing me, Liam rose to leave.

"No, stay, Liam. I might have use for you."

June ordered Liam to pour a cup of tea for me. "Some cakes?" she asked, looking amused.

I noticed that several buttons on her blouse were undone. Egads! "I'll have the pink ones."

Liam filled a plate with little frosted pink cakes and baby biscuits filled with sliced ham.

Abigail Keam

"Lovely," I replied, taking a sip of my tea. "I needed something."

"To what do we owe this visit? Not that I'm not thrilled to see you anytime," cooed June, looking smug.

Liam handed me a napkin.

"I need some information that only you can get for me, and perhaps you too, Liam."

June leaned forward. "I'm intrigued."

"For some reason the ATF is still making Shaneika's life miserable. They searched her home and office today."

"But why?" asked June, her hand on Liam's thigh. "I thought you said that Charlie wasn't in the gondola. It seems like they should be looking for Charlie. He has no connection with Shaneika other than they are in the racing business and committed a social gaffe at my party."

"It was terrible that those two ruined your Derby party, my Lady," interjected Liam before popping a baby cake topped with blue icing and sprinkles into his mouth.

I noticed that he had had some extensive cosmetic dental work done. No doubt a gift from June. She could not abide the European tendency for having bad teeth, one of her few American prejudices.

June smiled at Liam. "Charlie ruined it. Shaneika was just being Shaneika."

"I think Charlie specifically targeted Shaneika to make it look like they were having a feud."

"For what purpose?" inquired June, taking a sip of tea.

125

I reached for another biscuit. "To create smoke, a diversion. Besides scrutinizing Shaneika, the ATF also searched Charlie's house and office, taking everyone's computers. They are systemically going through all their leads."

"How do you want me to help?" asked June, looking adoringly at Liam who returned a wondrous smile, displaying his new teeth.

"First, put a cap on it both of you, will ya? Sober up. This is serious."

"Party pooper," replied June. "Whatever, go on."

"June, I need you to use your connections to find out if there was anything fishy with Charlie. Was he about to go bankrupt? Did he have a gambling problem?"

"That should be easy enough to do," mused June. "I'll make some calls and also ask some of the barn hands if they know something. They are huge gossips."

"What do you want me to do?" asked Liam, also intrigued.

"I'm sure you have made many nefarious acquaintances since you've been here. Make contact and see what they know."

"I've quit my bad ways, haven't I, Luv?"

I looked at June. "How many watches did he steal at the Derby?"

"Six . . . and two wallets . . . and one pair of ruby earrings."

"And I gave them all up, I did!"

126

June laughed. "Yes, after his day of fun, we turned everything in to the Lost and Found."

Liam looked earnestly at me. "Got to keep my hand in."

I nodded while rising. Without thinking, I checked to see if my watch was still on my wrist.

"Look, my Lady, she doesn't trust me."

"Neither do I. That's what makes you so irresistible, you bad, bad boy," cooed June.

Yuck!

I couldn't wait to get away from those two . . . but not before I pinched some more of those little cakes . . . and some biscuits . . . and some raspberry cookies that I hadn't tried. I was so laden down I could barely make my escape.

31

Two days later, Shaneika, Asa, and I were seated in the Big House's music room, sucking down bourbons.

It was eleven in the morning.

The three of us had spent those two days threatening, cajoling, snooping, and bribing anyone who could give us any information on Charlie Hoskins. Basically, we came up with a big fat zero, so we were drowning our sorrows.

Charlie's business was in okay shape–not great but solid. There were no sordid stories of messy love affairs. He didn't have an interest in women. And Franklin checked the other side of the fence for Charlie's love inclination. There was nothing. Charlie's big love was work.

He had no close friends as he had been an ass to everyone, but Charlie was respected in the community, if not liked, and seemed to be honest.

A big dead end.

June entered the library with Liam, her sidekick. Everywhere June went, Liam was right behind her.

It irritated me. Don't ask me why. It just did.

I scooted over on the couch to make room for June, but she chose to sit in a leather armchair.

Liam sat next to me. He smelled like expensive cologne and horses.

"We came up with zip," Asa said. "Charlie has simply vanished off the face of the earth."

June smiled. "In a week or so, I think you should start having your men check all the international flights, either to Switzerland or to the Caribbean, especially the Cayman Islands."

"That is where banks don't ask questions," replied Asa, "and all accounts have only numbers, not names."

"So you believe that Charlie is alive and on the run," I stated, looking between Liam and June.

Liam nodded.

"Why?" asked Shaneika.

"Everything Charlie did those few weeks leading up to and on the day of the Derby was to provide an alibi and focus wrong-doing on others such as Shaneika. Harassing Shaneika was done to provoke her into a public display of anger," commented June, studying Shaneika.

"Which I fell for," uttered Shaneika, looking sheepish.

"And then there was all that silly business with the two crews, two balloons, the explosion, and on and

on," continued June. "It was the explosion that really
interested me. No person or horse was hurt. Just a few
cars dented here and there. The explosion was all smoke
and mirrors. A big, loud boom to divert people's
attention from what was really going on.

"What nailed the explosion for us was that most of
the metal used in hot air balloons was replaced with
plastic or rope. The gondola itself was wicker."

"Exploding plastic can cause damage," countered
Asa, frowning.

"Yes, but not as much as metal," replied Liam. "It
was the lack of metal that pointed to the explosion as a
setup."

"How did you get a copy of the ATF report?" asked
Shaneika. "Even Asa couldn't finagle a copy."

"Simple," stated June. "I didn't. I just had some of
my workers talk with the ground crew at the Downs. I'm
telling you that house, hotel, and ground staff are all
gossips. They certainly know more about the people they
serve than the other way around."

"Yes," jumped in Liam, "we had our people talk with
workers who were doing cleanup and searching for
injured people before the police got there. They told our
people that no one was hurt and there was very little
debris. They were puzzled about the lack of detritus.
The explosion turned out to be a very loud bang and
some smoke, but that was all. They never saw anything
that remotely looked like human remains."

"So what are you saying?" I asked, somewhat impatiently. I already knew that stuff. I wanted to move on to something I didn't know.

"I'm not finished," fussed June. "I sent some of my groomers and hot walkers up to Pimlico. They found out that Persian Blue is still running in the race, even though Charlie is not around. Apparently Charlie was not the only owner of Persian Blue. There were several silent partners who have now stepped forward. But now, the crux of the matter."

"Yes, let's get to the point," encouraged Asa.

June smiled. "You're going to love this, Shaneika. My guys took Charlie's men out to a bar and got them stinking drunk. One of them said that he had overheard a vet tell Charlie that Persian Blue had a serious problem."

"What was it?" asked Shaneika, leaning forward in her chair.

June smirked. "It seems that Persian Blue had a very low sperm count."

Liam, positively twitching with glee, interrupted, "In other words, ladies, Persian Blue was shooting blanks."

Shaneika, Asa, and I looked at each other and muttered together, "Ahhhh."

32

In the Thoroughbred business, the real money is made from breeding your horse to other horses. The races are a way to increase the breeding fees. Winning more important races with larger purses is the way to increase a horse's stud fee.

A champion may race for only two or three years, but may live to be twenty years old. He may breed for ten to fifteen years, depending upon his health. And if that horse produced offspring that were winners too, the sky's the limit for the breeding fee. That sire would stand to make a fortune.

But if the horse's ability to reproduce is limited, then the horse is basically worthless after he stops racing. He is not worth anything to anyone even though he's a champion.

If it were true that Persian Blue was sterile, then we understood why Charlie flew the coop. He had already sold breeding shares to Persian Blue, which he would have to refund. Besides that, Charlie would be the laughing stock of the horse industry and the butt of many tasteless jokes.

Charlie's erratic behavior was beginning to make sense.

Asa looked at Shaneika. "Either Charlie has run off with the money or the money is no longer available to refund."

Shaneika poured another bourbon while directing a question at June. "Why did you say to look for him in a week or so?"

"That's when the bandages would need to come off," answered June.

Asa half-rose from her seat in excitement. "Plastic surgery!"

"You got it, kid," replied June. "His face is plastered on every agency's WANTED board. He could never get out of the country with that ugly mug of his."

Shaneika nodded in agreement. "So he would have to have his face altered. Why didn't I think of that?"

June waved for me to pour her a drink. "If I were you," she said to us all, "check all flights out. Also I would start looking in Miami. He would need to be close to a port. At this stage, it might still be uncomfortable to travel long distances, even with pain medication."

"And a cruise ship would be an ideal hiding place," I concurred. "They wouldn't be so strict about boarding as an airplane."

June looked rather pleased with herself. "I think sometime during one of the day trips, Charlie is going to jump ship and get on a little island hopper to some place where his syndicate buddies might not think to look."

"That still doesn't explain why the ATF is still after Shaneika," I said.

June looked at Asa. "I think Shaneika was used by Charlie as a smoke screen and Minor used them both to *smoke* out Asa. I think he wanted to see her again. Minor knew of Asa's close relationship Shaneika and used it to get Asa here."

"I am so tired of being used by people," snapped Shaneika, glaring at Asa. "You owe me, girlfriend."

"I acted exactly as Minor wanted," complained Asa. "As soon as I heard that Shaneika was in trouble, I got on a plane. I can't believe I was so stupid."

"You weren't. Remember, I called you. It's my fault," I remarked. "But you should have left when I wanted you to."

"You all figure this out," muttered Shaneika, rising from the couch. "I've got to get to Baltimore for the next race in the Triple Crown. Let me know how this works out."

"Thanks for letting us hold the bag!" shouted Asa after her.

"That reminds me," June said to Liam. "We need to be in Baltimore too."

Liam rose and helped June out of her chair. "All arrangements have been made, my Lady. Charles and Amelia are ready whenever you are."

June turned to Asa and me. "You two lock up when you finish here. See you in a couple of days, Josiah. Asa, I hope you're in London when I get back. Get that dreadful man out of your life once and for all."

Asa rose and went across the room. Kissing June on the cheek, she said, "Thank you, Lady Elsmere. That's sound advice."

I sputtered, "I've been telling you that. How come June gets a kiss and I get the kiss-off?"

June laughed. "Oh, Josiah, it's so easy to push your buttons. Stay well, my darlings. I love you both."

Asa saw them to the door where Charles, Amelia, and the Bentley waited for them. She watched until the car went down the driveway and out of sight.

She found me in the kitchen with Bess, packing food in a basket. "Mom, what are you doing?"

"Bess is closing the kitchen while June is gone and we both are taking perishables out of the fridge, so they won't go to waste."

"Do you really need two pies?"

"I don't have two pies. I have slices from two pies."

Asa looked in the basket. "Look at all this ham. You've got country ham and city ham both."

"No one said you had to eat any of this," I replied while spooning broccoli casserole into Tupperware. "You're just creating a fuss to avoid seeing Minor."

"Minor?" said Bess sharply. "Is that rat in town?"

"You're behind on your gossip, Bess," I said.

"Must be. No one told me about Minor."

Asa grabbed several oatmeal cookies as she went out the door. "I'm going. I'm going. I'll get this settled with him for once and for all."

Bess watched out the window as Asa left. "I hope she doesn't end up shooting him."

It just slipped out of my mouth. "Some rats deserve to die."

It was then that I knew I needed to see Goetz again. I needed to set things straight.

33

Goetz opened the door to his apartment. "This is a surprise."

"May I come in?" I asked.

"Sure," he replied, stepping out of the way.

I entered his apartment and sat in a chair.

"Can I take your coat?" he asked.

"No, thanks. I'm not staying."

"Oh, I see. Are you going to tell me to get lost?"

"I've been thinking about what you told me and I wanted to assure you that is one secret I'll carry to my grave."

"That's nice," replied Goetz, taking a chair across from mine. "It would be hard to go to prison at my age . . . and a cop at that."

Goetz' face remained stoic, making it hard to read him. I continued, "I wanted to thank you for saving me. I am truly grateful."

Goetz nodded. "It sounds like there is a 'but' coming somewhere in this."

"You said that when Minor married Asa, you checked us out. Brannon and I were already in a rocky place then. I think that is when he started hiding money from me. Would you know where he put it?"

Goetz hesitated for a moment and then answered, "I might."

I rubbed my hands together from sheer nervousness. "Brannon sold his share of his architectural firm and received five hundred thousand dollars. I never saw a penny of that money."

"Is this what you came here to discuss? Money? What about us?"

"There is no 'us'. There never was an 'us'."

"So what were we doing?"

"Two lonely people spending some quality time together. It was never more than friendship."

"Maybe on your part."

"I told you that I was finished with love and love was finished with me."

"You never gave us a chance."

"Are you going to tell me where Brannon stashed that money?"

"No," he answered flatly.

"No?"

"No."

"Why won't you tell me?"

"You want to know why Jake really left?"

I shook my head. "I'm not here to discuss Jake."

"Because for the longest time, you had Brannon's ashes in your closet. Your closet! Then you have Brannon's pictures all over the Butterfly . . . still. After all the crap he gave you, there are pictures of him everywhere. Who can compete with a dead man?"

"I loved Brannon. He built the Butterfly for me."

"And took credit for your design and then made you suffer for his deception."

"It wasn't like that."

Goetz shook his head. "Yes, it was, Josiah. Your faith in that man was completely misplaced and deep down you know it.

"Your daughter knew about Brannon. That's one of the reasons she left after high school. She might not have known any of the details, but she knew there was something phony about her old man, and she didn't want to be witness to it anymore."

"That's a lie. Asa loved Brannon."

"Maybe, but did Brannon love Asa? Did he stick by Asa during the trial?"

I cradled my head in my hands, remembering that awful night when Brannon left me.

Asa's life was being ripped apart. Brannon and I were drowning in debt and he took that moment to leave during dinner, taking my good jewelry, some of my couture dresses, and my dignity with him.

It only took Asa a few moments to discover that Brannon had drained our bank accounts as well.

Goetz was right.

Brannon had been an awful man–beautiful on the outside, but so ugly on the inside.

I just hadn't been able to face the fact that I had been so gullible. Oh, over the years, I had come close to admitting it, but not really owning it.

Now the truth smacked me right in the face.

And there was no running away from it now.

But I was going to try.

34

I rushed to the door, but Goetz moved more quickly than I did.

He slammed the door shut.

I wouldn't look at him.

"Don't go, Josiah," Goetz whispered in my ear. "Take a chance. Spend the night with me."

He pulled me to him and kissed me softly on the lips, and then my face and neck.

I pushed away from him, but the man was incredibly strong.

Goetz held me tighter.

"I don't trust you," I protested.

"So don't trust me," Goetz whispered. He began to nuzzle my neck.

I'm ashamed to say that it felt nice. I'm ashamed to say that I raised my head to meet his lips. I'm ashamed to say that I returned his kiss.

I'm just ashamed.

35

I have only had three lovers in my life. A boyfriend in my first year of college. Oh my, how we fumbled with each other.

Then Brannon. He was already experienced. Even during our low points, I always enjoyed our private time together.

Then there was Jake. We were so in sync that being with Jake was a sublime experience. Jake was a drug for me–a big bag of painkillers. I actually went into withdrawal when he went away. I miss him every day, with every breath I take. It's another kind of pain that I have to get used to.

Three? Just three. What about Matt? You know that Matt and I played that silly game where we acted like lovers just to give the neighbors something to gossip about.

Yes, I did go to his house that night. And yes, being with Matt was my intention. I'm not making excuses for my bad judgment, but I was out of my mind. My regret is that I put Matt in a bind.

Oh, he tried to accommodate me, but it was a disaster. I started giggling at the absurdity of us together and after that, Matt lost his will or his nerve. I don't know which.

We ended up in bed, watching old movies and I fell asleep with a bowl of popcorn on my lap and Matt snoring beside me.

Why have I let Franklin think differently all these years?

If you remember, I tried to tell him nothing happened. It was then that I realized Franklin would never believe the truth, so I lied and took the blame.

It was better to let him think the worst of me and then move on . . . which he never did.

But I deserved whatever Franklin hurled at me.

I was wrong to go to Matt. I know that.

As for Goetz, I'm not ready to go there yet.

I'm still very confused.

36

Minor was tired as he climbed into his rented SUV. All he wanted to do was go to the hotel, take a hot shower, and have a steak. He turned around to look over his shoulder so he could back out, but then uttered a small cry. "Mary, Jesus, and Joseph!" he snapped. "You scared the bejeebies out of me."

"Aren't you supposed to look in the back seat before you open your car door?" replied Asa.

"What do you want?"

"Let's go somewhere we can talk."

"You carrying?"

"The same as you, so that makes us even. If I had wanted to kill you, I would have done so by now."

"Just talk?"

"Just talk."

"Where?"

"Somewhere that we won't be observed."

"I prefer some place public."

Asa pursed her lips. "I thought we had kissed and made-up."

"Yeah, right. A little sex between us doesn't smooth out all the wrinkles."

"Don't be such a drama queen. Let's go."

Minor hesitated.

"I insist, Minor."

Recognizing Asa's steely tone of voice, Minor pulled out of the parking lot and headed for his hotel. He wondered if she wanted a replay of last week. If so, Minor was up for it. He enjoyed sex with Asa, but she could just as easily put a bullet through his skull. That's what made her so exciting.

One never knew with Asa.

37

"Pull over here," insisted Asa.

That was fine with Minor. They were on Short Street in the restaurant district. Lots of bright lights and people walking the street.

"Let's get out," directed Asa.

Minor parked the car, looking around. He got out and followed Asa to a bar where she sat in a café chair on the sidewalk.

"Sit down, Minor," she said, after ordering two drinks.

Minor reluctantly sat in the chair opposite her. "Okay, I'm here. Let's make this quick. I'm tired and want to go to my hotel."

Asa brushed his concerns aside. "I think it's time that you answered some questions."

"It's a little late for the truth, isn't it?" Minor started to get out of his chair.

"Sit back down, Minor."

"Why?"

"See that man over there?" Asa nodded toward a large man dressed in black, holding a newspaper in front of him. "He's got a gun pointed at you behind that paper. Now, he's not going to kill you, but shoot you in the leg. It will hurt like hell and be a huge inconvenience. You surely don't want that."

Minor eased back into his seat, staring at the man wearing black sunglasses.

"A shot will surely cause a commotion, Asa."

"I'll be walking away while people are trying to figure out why you are screaming for help as no one will hear the shot." Asa leaned forward and whispered, "My friend's gun has a silencer. If you try to run away, he will shoot. If you cause a scene, he will shoot."

Minor looked around. Beads of sweat were faintly visible on his forehead.

"Don't even think about running back to your car. It's gone. Probably in your hotel parking lot by now, but out of your reach."

A waiter approached their table and served their drinks.

Minor tried to get his attention, but failed. Resigned, Minor picked up his drink and took a sip. "Your guy?"

"Yep."

"Well, it seems I'm a captive date. What do you want?"

"I want to know why you turned on me."

"Ah, geez. Old history. Let it stay buried. We got a divorce, didn't we?"

Asa continued, "I trusted you. I believed in you."

"You trusted me? You didn't trust me. That was the problem," Minor answered heatedly. "You got this bug up your ass about a few lousy agents and went flapping your jaws to the Washington Post."

"They were putting people's lives in danger. How can you condone their behavior?"

"You don't listen. I never condoned their behavior, but you didn't see the big picture. Everything is black and white to you."

"You should have watched my back, Minor."

Minor shook his head. "This is what you don't get. You were on your way to the top. You were headed for the very apex of the organization. There you could have made a difference, cleaned out the corruption, fired the incompetent, but you didn't have the patience to wait. All you had to do was keep your nose clean and your head down.

"Ten years down the road you could have made an impact within the department with no scandal, but noooo, you had to make a big splash. All over the newspapers. You think those guys are gonna take it lying down? They're gonna come back at you and hard, baby."

"How did they get you to put drugs in my car? Did they threaten you? Did you take money to throw your wife under the bus?"

"Let's get everything out on the table. Is that what this is all about? Yeah, I put those drugs in your car. You were one step away from getting your head blown off. They were going to stop you one way or another."

Asa's face quivered with anger. "You shit. You almost got me sent to prison."

"I saved your life, you stupid broad," hissed Minor. "I was stalling for time. I knew that if I put you back in the national limelight, they would think twice about you having a fatal accident. By the time your trial was over, they had already been investigated and terminated from the department. They had nothing to gain by going after you then. They were disgraced, but you were neutralized. The score was even."

"Not only did you ruin me professionally and tainted my reputation, you ruined my parents' marriage."

"Ruin you? You have your own international security company. You are called in on the most delicate and sensitive cases. I didn't ruin you. I made you!"

Asa stared at Minor. "Why did you leave me?"

"You left me, remember. You accused me of putting those drugs in your car and said you never wanted to see me again. You wouldn't give me a chance to explain."

"That's not how I remember it."

"Of course not. You're never wrong." Minor stood. "I've had enough of this. I did what I did to save you. I was older, wiser, but you were always so headstrong, you wouldn't listen. I told you that going to the Washington

Post was going to open up a floodgate that you wouldn't be able to close. I told you that your identity would be compromised and it was. I told you that everyone around you would be affected, and we were. Maybe when you're older, you'll understand. You're still very young."

He threw some money on the table. "I'm going to walk back to my hotel now. It's a nice night for a stroll."

"One more thing?"

Minor wearily sighed. "What?"

"Why did you go after Shaneika?"

"Purely selfish on my part. I wanted to see you."

"Now that you've seen me?"

"You're still the most beautiful woman I have ever known."

"Did you love me, Minor?"

"Baby, I've never stopped."

38

Boris put down his newspaper and walked over to Asa, watching Minor disappear around the corner. "You want me to follow him?"

Asa shook her head.

"You find out what you wanted?"

"I don't know if I should believe him." Asa brushed away a tear and laughed nervously. "I'm certainly my mother's daughter–headstrong, self-righteous. I was so sure I was doing the right thing back then."

"Now you not so sure."

Asa looked at Boris. There was doubt in her eyes. "What if Minor is right? What if I was a fool?"

"He's not right. You took a stand against evil, but the cost was more than you . . . how you say?"

"Bargained for?"

"Yes, bargain for, but that doesn't mean you were wrong."

Asa gave a weak smile. "Thanks for trying to cheer me up, Boris."

"Let's go to your mother's house. I want to see big slobbery dog again."

Asa brightened. "I know for a fact that she has lots of food. Mom cleaned out Lady Elsmere's fridge."

"Good. I'm hungry."

As Boris and Asa started for his rented car, they didn't see that Minor had doubled back and was watching them from across the street.

Minor grinned. Tell a woman she's beautiful and she'll fall for it every time.

It was just a matter of time until he got what he wanted from Asa.

39

I was selling honey at the Farmers' Market when Goetz showed up.

"What kind of honey is this? Looks like water," he said, holding a bottle up to the light.

"It's Locust honey."

"Why's it so light?"

"The bees gather nectar from the Black Locust tree when it blossoms in May. The nectar turns into a honey that is light in color and very sweet."

Goetz pulled ten dollars out of his wallet and handed the money to me. "The official report about the balloon explosion came out."

"And?"

"It is considered a suspicious bombing with no casualties by person or persons unknown."

"Accident was ruled out, huh?"

"Yep, and you will be pleased to know that no agency will be contacting Shaneika about it in the future. She's been scratched off the list."

"So, is Charlie Hoskins still alive then?"

"There's that possibility, but no one has seen him since the morning of the Derby. He could be lying in a shallow grave somewhere."

"What's your take on him?"

"I think Charlie is probably in Brazil or France. Some country that doesn't have an extradition treaty with the US."

Goetz and I stared at each other for a moment and then broke out laughing.

"All this over a horse who is sterile," I said, gaining my composure. "Those investors lost their money. I feel sorry for them."

If Goetz was surprised that I knew about Persian Blue, he didn't show it. "Yeah, my heart bleeds for those rich bastards."

"Did you know that Persian Blue was infertile before the story broke on the news?"

Goetz rubbed his chin. "There were rumors and then Minor interviewed the horse's vet who spilled the beans. After we knew that, Charlie's actions made sense. Take the money and run."

"If Persian Blue loses the Preakness, he'll be considered a lame duck."

"He'll be sold to a dog food company after he finishes his tour regardless."

I shook my head. "No, Lady Elsmere is going to purchase him when his price hits bottom dollar and let him live out his life on her farm. It isn't Persian Blue's fault that he can't reproduce. He's still a great racehorse and that should be respected."

"I tip my hat to Lady Elsmere then. That's a decent thing to do."

I shifted uncomfortably, having run out of things to say.

"I'll be going then," Goetz declared.

"Sure."

Goetz turned to leave.

"Hey, Goetz," I said.

He swiveled around.

"We okay?"

Goetz' hounddog face drooped. "Yeah, we're okay. See ya."

"See ya," I said.

As I watched Goetz walk away, I wondered if I had made the right decision.

40

Boris slipped a pair of binoculars out of his coat pocket. Looking through them, he spotted his quarry. Handing the binoculars to Asa, he said, "Three o'clock. Checked shorts, straw hat."

Asa located Minor and his partner, Joseph Caperella, boarding a cruise ship in Miami. "Minor's wearing Bermuda shorts," jeered Asa. "He looks like a dork."

"What's dork?" asked Boris.

"A nerd."

Boris shrugged. "I have shorts like his. I see nothing bad about them."

Asa handed the binoculars back to Boris. "Then I should take you shopping."

"Shopping with you? A woman who wears nothing but black? I should go shopping with you?"

"Somehow I don't think that was a compliment. What color would you like to see me in?"

Boris gave Asa the once-over. "Something bright and cheerful. Maybe a gold or a soft pink."

"Pink? You're pushing it there, boy."

"Something besides black. It's depressing."

"You wear black."

"I am man. I am the muscle. Black is masculine."

"You are forty years behind the times is what you are."

Boris harrumphed. Turning his attention back to the cruise ship, he asked, "Are we to board?"

"No. We have plenty of agents on board to keep tabs on Minor. They'll notify us when they catch Minor putting the make on Charlie Hoskins."

"It was clever of you to put tracking device in Minor's wallet, or we'd not know that he got a lead on Hoskins."

"He always took long showers. Gave me enough time to go through his wallet. You know where I put it? He still had a picture of me. I put that dot on my eye. He would have to be looking for it to discover that it is there."

"GPS that small?"

"Classified really. Still experimental. An Army general owed me a favor."

"Ah," commented Boris. He was quiet and then asked, "Minor still had picture of you?"

"Funny, huh?" Out of the corner of her eye, Asa caught a glimpse of the dock security heading for their car. "Let's go. We'll catch a plane to the Caymans and be there before the ship docks. I want to witness Minor taking Charlie down."

"Then what?" asked Boris, putting the car in gear and driving away. They headed toward the airport.

"Then I contact one of Charlie's partners and let them know that Charlie and the money have been found. I'll let nature take its course."

"I don't understand."

"I've got an inside contact with the Cayman police. As soon as Charlie is arrested, I'll know the numbers to his account and the amount. What I'm interested in is that all the money in the account is taken into evidence."

"You think Minor will skim some off the top."

"I've always wondered how dirty Minor was. Now is my chance. He doesn't think anyone is watching."

Boris looked at Asa with admiration. "So if money is missing, then the syndicate for Persian Blue will put two and two together."

"And since many of them are from New Jersey, I believe they will take matters into their own hands."

"You would do this to a man you once loved?" questioned Boris.

"I've always wondered who leaked my name to the press. In the back of my mind it was never anyone from the Washington Post. I've always suspected it was Minor."

"Why would he do such bad thing?"

"Power, Boris. He made a trade and I was the bargaining chip."

"You don't know."

"No, but I'm getting close to finding out the answer."

Asa watched Boris drive. "I hope I'm wrong, Boris. But something in my gut tells me my hunch is right."

"Too bad."

"Why do you say that?"

"A husband should protect his wife. That's his duty. I would always protect my woman first."

"I believe you, Boris. You're a good man. I'm glad you're my partner in this."

Boris shot Asa a quick smile. "Maybe in the Caymans, we go shopping. I pick out an outfit for you and you pick out an outfit for me."

Asa didn't reply.

"What's the matter? You think I pick out something ugly?"

"No, it's that I haven't contemplated doing something fun for the longest time. I wouldn't know how to act."

"After Hoskins is arrested, we stay on the island for a few days. Unwind. Eat. Sleep. Dance. Enjoy life a little."

Asa thought for a moment. Should she?

She was tired and needed to rest. And she would feel more comfortable if she had Boris to watch her back.

Finally, she said, "Yes, let's do, but do me a favor. Don't tell my mother."

41

And where was the man who had caused all this turmoil and excitement?

Was Charlie in Rio?

Was Charlie in a pine box buried somewhere in the forests near Louisville?

Was Charlie sleeping with the catfish in the Ohio River?

No.

Charlie was alive and well, dressed in a loud yellow Hawaiian shirt and sandals with white socks, catching a cab to the Port of Miami.

42

Charlie Hoskins was a happy man.

His plan had worked. Even though he wanted to smile at the man who checked his passport, he couldn't. His face was too tight and raw from the reconstruction.

Passing into the main lobby of the ship, Charlie glanced in a mirror. Again, Charlie smiled inwardly. His own mother wouldn't recognize him.

Someone bumped into him, which caused Charlie to groan. He needed to get to his stateroom fast and take more pain medication. With a map of the ship and his key card in hand, Charlie finally made the way to his suite.

Throwing himself on the bed, Charlie delighted in his luxurious surroundings. He began to chuckle, but stopped when that caused a spasm of pain.

Charlie hurriedly unzipped his bag and opened a vial containing pain medication. He popped several pills and swallowed them with the champagne he discovered on the nightstand beside his bed. There was also a basket full of chocolates to accompany the fruit and muffin tray.

Charlie sighed. He had worked hard for decades, but never achieved the monetary success he felt he deserved. Only when he discovered that Persian Blue was shooting blanks did Charlie concoct a plan to live the life he always wanted. And he had gotten away with it too.

Ever since that fateful day when the vet told Charlie the results of Persian Blue's fertility test, Charlie began planning his escape. He transferred most of the syndicate's money to an untraceable account in the Caribbean. Then he found a plastic surgeon with a gambling problem, who was happy to be paid in cash.

The hardest part was to plan his getaway from Kentucky to Miami. He staged it during the Kentucky Derby where his associates would be so sloshed with Mint Juleps and partying with their friends, they wouldn't investigate the balloon explosion until after the Derby race.

His only regret is that he didn't see Persian Blue run the Kentucky Derby in person. He saw the race later on YouTube.

Charlie teared at the thought of his beloved horse. That sacrifice was almost too much to bear.

If only Persian Blue had been whole. Things would have turned out much differently. But they hadn't and Charlie accepted that fact, even if he didn't like it.

The money would make up for his disappointment.

43

"This is like finding a needle in a haystack," grumbled Joe Caperella to Minor. "There is no one aboard this ship that looks like Charlie Hoskins."

"We assumed that Charlie had his face redone, so look for someone with his body type with a red face and fresh scars," replied Minor, sucking on a rum punch with a colorful paper umbrella in the glass.

Both men were ensconced near the pool, pretending to play gin rummy.

Joe looked around the pool area. "I see lots of short, fat men with red faces. This is next to impossible."

Minor put down a card. "If we can't identify him on the ship, we have agents staked out at the banks when we dock tomorrow. We'll catch Charlie Hoskins sooner or later."

Joe picked a card up from the stack and looked at it.

Grimacing, he threw it down.

Minor quickly picked it up and playfully announced, "Gin!"

44

Boris and Asa were on the trail of Minor, who was following a man he thought might be Charlie Hoskins. The man had hairline scars on his face and he had stayed in his cabin most of the cruise except for this port of call. Now this man was going straight to a bank.

Minor sat across from the bank in a little café. He spoke into a lapel microphone. "If the man in the green parrot shirt withdraws a lot of cash, pick him up outside the bank for questioning."

Asa and Boris followed suit and sat at an outdoor bar where they had a view of both Minor and the bank. Even if Minor had looked in their direction, he never would have recognized Asa. She was wearing resort clothes with ample padding underneath and a gray wig. Boris was also gray and hunched over. They looked like an average retired couple on their first voyage.

"Is this what you meant by shopping for new outfits?" kidded Boris, glancing at Asa. "You look old."

"Thanks. I worked hard on the makeup," replied Asa.

"I don't mean that in a good way," mumbled Boris, looking away.

"What did you say?"

"Nothing."

A waiter came over. Boris ordered some drinks and appetizers.

They were pretending to look at timeshare brochures when all hell broke loose across the street.

The man with a green parrot shirt came out of the bank with a briefcase and was accosted by three men. He was thrown to the ground and handcuffed.

During the scuffle, the parrot man dropped his briefcase, which popped open when it fell.

Both Asa and Boris rose from their seats to get a better view. Asa made visual contact with her agent stationed outside the bank, who began discreetly filming the incident, including the contents of the briefcase. "Is there money?" she texted.

"Sí," was the reply.

"We have it!" she gleefully exclaimed. She began dialing a number. "Now to download the file and send it."

Boris grabbed her hand. "You need to think about what you are doing. You want revenge on a husband who betrayed you. I understand. But you loved this man once. If you go through with this, you will never be rid of him. If the syndicate kills him, you will feel guilty the rest of your life. If he gets away with his schemes, then you will be angry and resentful the rest of your life. Either let him go or I go over to his table right now and shoot him in the head."

"If I ordered you to execute Minor, you would do it?" asked Asa.

"Yes, but better to let him go. Better for you. Better for him."

Asa stared at her cell phone and then up at Boris, who looked so painfully sincere. Reluctantly, she pushed the end button.

Smiling, she pulled off her wig. "Louie, I think this is the beginning of a beautiful friendship."

"That's a line from movie we saw other night."

"Yes, it is. Let's go shopping, Boris. Then we can lunch down by the beach. It's such a lovely day in Paradise. Let's not waste it."

Asa wrapped her hand around Boris' forearm, and together they left the bar, headed toward the shopping district.

As they passed by a waste barrel, Asa threw her phone in it.

Epilogue

So that's how Charlie Hoskins soared to the heights of the Thoroughbred racing industry, and like Icarus, fell back to Earth.

After the dust settled, Mike asked Shaneika out on an official date. To my surprise, she accepted. They had a nice time.

Asa spent a month in the Caribbean, taking a long deserved vacation. Then she got called about a museum robbery in Milan. The money was too good to pass up, so she accepted the job and handled it herself rather than sending one of her people. She took Boris with her. Wonder what's going on there.

Kelly went back to his wife with his tail tucked between his legs. That's where he belongs. They are working on their marriage.

I went to see his wife. If she knows about Asa, she's not spilling. I hope she doesn't because Kelly loves her and if they get over this bump, they will have a wonderful life together.

I am resigned to the fact that you don't always get what you want, but if you try, sometimes you find you get what you need. Gee, that sounds like Rolling Stone wisdom.

Oh, you want to know which horse won the Kentucky Derby!

Simply turn the page.

This is how it went down.

And they are in the gate and . . .
THEY'RE OFF FOR THE KENTUCKY DERBY!

Bold Forbes on the far outside.

Whirlaway is caught behind and now trailing.

Tim Tam in front.

Persian Blue moving up on the inside.

Comanche trailing last.

Whirlaway in a world of trouble, caught behind the pack,
now moving on the outside.

Comanche, Pink Star, and Hill Gail last
as they approach the Clubhouse turn.

It's Tim Tam first, Bold Forbes second, and Swale third
with Persian Blue moving fast on the inside.

Burgoo King is making his move, right behind Persian
Blue.

Coming 'round the half-mile post, it is still Tim Tam first, Bold Forbes second, and Swale with Persian Blue now tied for third.

Vagrant is fifth and Sir Barton sixth.

Pink Star is trailing, but making strides. Pink Star now has passed Vagrant and moving to the inside.

Sir Barton is picking it up and passing Vagrant.

Wait! Wait! The black stallion, Comanche, is making a move and pushing his way through. Past Hill Gail! Past Whirlaway! He is bounding past Ben Brush and Baden-Baden! The crowd is going wild.

Tim Tam still first, but Persian Blue is moving past Bold Forbes.

They're approaching the final stretch.

Persian Blue, the four white stocking favorite, is neck and neck with Tim Tam, but wait . . . I can't believe it– Comanche is flying like the wind, coming up fast.

The crowd is on its feet and screaming like I've never heard them.

Comanche has passed Bold Forbes.

In two lengths, Persian Blue has passed Tim Tam and is now making his bid for the Kentucky Derby.

Persian Blue has pulled out ahead of Tim Tam!

Comanche has now passed Tim Tam!

Comanche is challenging Persian Blue, the favorite. The crowd is beyond wild. I can't believe it myself!

Persian Blue and Comanche are neck and neck. They are now in the final furlong. Persian Blue and Comanche are giving it their all. As they turn for home, Persian Blue and Comanche are deadlocked, neck and neck.

Further back Bold Forbes is third with Tim Tam following close.

Tim Tam is fading fast!

Persian Blue and Comanche in front battling it out. It's going to be close with Persian Blue by a nose . . . by the tip of a nose. Folks, it's that close.

PERSIAN BLUE AND COMANCHE LEAVING EVERYONE IN THE DUST!

WHAT A RACE! I CAN'T BELIVE IT!

PERSIAN BLUE AND COMANCHE FIGHTING TO THE BITTER END!

PERSIAN BLUE AND COMANCHE NECK AND NECK!

IT WILL BE A PHOTO FINISH, BUT THE WINNER OF THE KENTUCKY DERBY IS PERSIAN BLUE BY A NOSE.

COMANCHE SECOND AND BOLD FORBES THIRD FOLLOWING SEVERAL LENGTHS BEHIND.

PERSIAN BLUE IS THE WINNER OF THE KENUCKY DERBY!

Doesn't that suck? By a nose! Really? Well, no use crying over spilt milk.

It's on to the Preakness Stakes in Maryland.

MY OLD KENTUCKY HOME
Words and Music by Stephen Foster
As sung on Kentucky Derby Day

The sun shines bright in the old Kentucky home
'Tis summer, the people are gay;
The corn top's ripe and the meadow's in the bloom,
While the birds make music all the day;
The young folks roll on the little cabin floor,
All merry, all happy, and bright,
By'n by hard times comes a-knocking at the door,
Then my old Kentucky home, good night!

Chorus
Weep no more, my lady,
Oh weep no more today!
We will sing one song for the old Kentucky home,
For the old Kentucky home far away.

BONUS CHAPTERS

<u>Last Chance Motel</u>
A Romance Novel

Last Chance Motel

1

Eva gazed into the floor-length mirror and was pleased with her reflection. The black negligee she had recently purchased encased her trim body like a glove. Her auburn hair glimmered with highlights and her skin looked like butter cream. Even though she was forty, Eva looked younger and worked at it.

Hoping that her sexy look might heat up her husband, who seemed a little frost-bitten lately, she put on the finishing touch. Passion Fire Red lipstick!

Nine years ago, she had met Dennis while helping his company remodel an old warehouse on the west side of Manhattan. Her boss had put Eva in charge of the cosmetic rehab of the warehouse while others dealt with structural issues. That was okay with Eva. Buying furniture and picking out paint colors was fun and she was given a huge budget with which to play.

It was at a briefing that Eva was introduced to Dennis, a junior executive at that time. He was to be the company's liaison with her.

There was instant chemistry and before long they were embroiled in a passionate affair, which spilled over into marriage two months after the project was completed.

Nine years. Eva shook her head in disbelief. Where had the time gone? Six of those years had been fantastic, but things started slipping three years ago.

It had begun when Eva and Dennis purchased an abandoned brownstone in Brooklyn near the Verrazano Bridge. They had been giddy when they first received the keys from the bank and began restoring the four-story brownstone, but things started taking a downward turn six months into the project.

To save money, Eva and Dennis decided to complete many of the cosmetic projects themselves. After working long hours at their firms, they would hurry home to the brownstone and work late into the night trying to tile the bathrooms or lay down bamboo floors or paint twelve foot ceilings. What started as fun became a strain both physically and mentally.

They began snapping at each other and it didn't take long to realize that they both had different visions for the brownstone, which created even more tension.

Eva wanted to restore the brownstone to its authentic former glory while Dennis wanted to gut and modernize it completely.

Dennis won.

When the brownstone was completed, Eva had to admit it was stunning, complete with all modern amenities. But to Eva, the brownstone was cold and void of any personality, but it was what Dennis liked. She disliked the cold paint colors he had chosen and the minimalist look of each room.

Eva realized that compromise was the cornerstone of marriage and wanted Dennis to be happy. That was very important to her. She could live with the renovation.

Now that the brownstone was finished, Eva wanted to heat up her faltering relationship with her husband and get it back on track.

Eva masked her irritation when Dennis finally got home . . . late as usual during the past seven months. Hearing the elevator rise to the master bedroom floor, Eva waited in the alcove trying to look sexy in her negligee.

The elevator reached the top and the door swung open. Dennis was going through the mail and barely looked up.

"Hello there, big boy," teased Eva.

Dennis looked up and froze when he saw Eva.

Eva noticed his hesitation and it threw her off her game. She suddenly felt foolish.

"What's up with you?" asked Dennis.

Eva, determined that the night be a success, smiled. "I thought we would celebrate your new promotion and the completion of the house. I have made a very nice dinner for us."

"We celebrated last Saturday with our friends," retorted Dennis. He looked frustrated and a bit embarrassed.

"Yes, but I thought we could have a private celebration, just you and me," rejoined Eva.

Uh oh. This was not going as planned.

"Honey, I'm tired. I just want to eat and go to bed."

"Long day at the office?"

Dennis looked at the letters in his hand. His face was flushed. "Something like that."

"I have something that will make you feel better," chirped Eva. She was going to hit this out of the ballpark. Eva handed him two airline tickets.

"What's this?" Dennis asked, staring blankly at the tickets.

"I purchased two tickets to Miami for this weekend. The two of us on a getaway. No work. No house to think about. Just warm breezes and blue water. We can rent a boat."

"NO!"

"No?" echoed Eva. Her heart began to sink. Something was very wrong.

"This has got to end," Dennis said, cutting in, letting the mail fall to the floor. He looked at Eva as though he was looking through her. "I'm sorry I have let this go on for so long, but things have got to change."

Alarmed, Eva tried to hug Dennis but he pushed her away. Eva gasped. "What is it, Dennis? What's wrong? Are you ill?" She felt a numbing fear move up her spine.

"I'm sorry, Eva, but I'm not going anywhere with you. This is very hard to say but I–I want a divorce."

Eva felt like a bullet had passed through her. "What? For heaven's sake, why? We have everything. We worked so hard on this house. Why Dennis? Why?"

"I don't love you anymore. That's why."

2

"Mr. Reardon wants the brownstone," demanded Dennis' lawyer.

Eva and her attorney sat across the conference table. "Where is Dennis?" Eva asked. Turning to her lawyer, she questioned, "Shouldn't Dennis be here?"

"Mr. Reardon has given me instructions to act on his behalf and feels his presence is not necessary under the circumstances."

"What circumstances? Not seeing me?" Eva asked.

"Eva," cautioned her lawyer. "Let me handle this."

"What circumstances are you referring to?" Eva asked again.

"I believe that Mr. Reardon has expressed concern about you being abusive lately."

Eva snorted in derision.

"Many women become upset when asked for a divorce and given no reason. Mrs. Reardon has been a faithful and constant companion to Mr. Reardon. I think that under the circumstances most women would raise their voices and maybe even throw some objects. It's human nature."

"Mr. Reardon feared for his life."

"Oh, please," scoffed Eva. "Give me a break."

"If Mr. Reardon feared for his safety he should have called the police and filed a complaint. Since there is no complaint, let's move on, shall we. Alleging that Mrs. Reardon is a threat without proof is counter-productive to your client's requests."

"Demands," rebuffed Dennis' lawyer.

"What are they?" asked Eva's attorney, putting a pencil to a legal pad.

"Quite simply, Mr. Reardon wants the brownstone." Dennis' attorney raised his hand. "I have been authorized to offer eight hundred thousand for your half, Mrs. Reardon, plus half of all moneyed accounts that you share with Mr. Reardon. I think it is a very equitable division of assets."

"I don't understand why Dennis would want the brownstone. It's too large for one person. I thought we were going to sell it and divide the proceeds," remarked Eva.

"They think that they . . .." The lawyer stopped suddenly, looking aghast at his faux pas.

"They?" questioned Eva.

"I meant he," stated Dennis' lawyer.

"You said 'they'."

Shaken, Eva leaned back in her seat. "They. That explains a lot. It's the missing piece of the puzzle of why he left me." She began to sob quietly.

Her lawyer closed his notebook. "Tell Mr. Reardon that Mrs. Reardon wants 1.2 million plus half of all the other assets or we are going to drag this out indefinitely."

"Oh no, you can't do that," complained Dennis' attorney. "The house needs to be available by the next several months before the due date."

Both Eva and her lawyer's mouth dropped open at the implication of the statement.

Eva began to wail out loud.

Her lawyer stood and helped Eva to her feet. "I assume that Mr. Reardon's new friend is pregnant then. He'll meet our demands or I'll tie up that brownstone for years."

"Oh God," whispered Eva, being led from the conference room. "He's got a new woman and they're going to have a baby in my house. My house! I painted every room! I installed the tile! I refinished the wood floors!" She yelled, "This just went from bad to the absolute worst. He told me he didn't want any children." Eva grabbed a woman in the hallway. "He said he would love me forever."

"They all say that, dearie. But if they can afford it, they trade us in every ten years or so for a new model. Once the tits start to sag, it's over," replied the stranger in sympathy. "We've all been there. It's just your turn now."

"What happened to true love?" murmured Eva.

Her lawyer snickered. "Surely you don't believe in that crap, do you? Just get the money and run."

"But I do. I do believe in true love," blurted Eva and she cried this mantra all the way home, that night and for the next several days until her body became so dehydrated she couldn't cry anymore.

3

Three months later, Eva signed the divorce papers and slipped them in the stamped mailer as directed. Licking the flap, she closed the mailer with a large sigh. "Well, that's the end of that," she said.

She hurried downstairs so she could catch the mailman whose truck she saw from the window. She caught him coming up the stoop and handed him the mailer.

Giving her a startled look, the mailman grabbed the envelope and hustled down the steps.

"I'm not that bad," she groused, noticing his reluctance to stay and chat.

A mother pushing a stroller hurried by when the toddler saw Eva and started to cry.

"Oh, come on now," complained Eva. Defeated, she pulled back inside the brownstone and looked in the hall mirror. "Jeez." Eva tried to flatten messy hair that would give Medusa a run for her money. Her eyes were sunken, teeth were yellow and dirty, and her skin was sallow.

Her outfit was pajamas that had not left Eva's body for the past two weeks and were straining at the seams as her new diet consisted of chocolate ice cream . . . and then strawberry ice cream . . . and again chocolate ice cream. With chocolate syrup. For a dessert, she inhaled Reddi-wip from the can.

And she stank.

"I'm in some deep, deep doo-doo," lamented Eva looking in the mirror and repelled by what she saw. "You're made of better stuff than this. You're just forty. Only six months ago you were hot stuff." She pulled on her belly fat. "Crap. I'm middle-aged now. The bloom has faded."

She gave the mirror one last pathetic look. "I just can't stop living. This is just a bump in the road." She took another hard look at herself. "Oh, who am I kidding? This is a freakin' firestorm!"

Coming to the realization that she had to battle her depression, Eva climbed the staircase to the third floor. There she took a long shower, washed her hair, shaved her legs and put on some clean underwear. Looking around the bedroom, she found a pair of clean flannel pj's and a tee shirt. To complete the outfit, she slipped on some beat-up flip-flops.

Hungry, she went to the kitchen, but found nothing in the fridge to eat. Frustrated, she began looking for carryout menus when she spotted the airline tickets to Florida.

Eva bit her lip as tears clouded her eyes. "I'm not going to cry," she whispered. "All that is over. I'm going to buck up and get over this. I'm going to get a new life." Staring at the plane tickets, Eva suddenly called her travel agent and ordered a new ticket to be waiting for her at the airport. Then Eva grabbed her coat and purse as she fled the brownstone.

Giving the brownstone one last look, Eva flipped the house key down a street grate.

Dennis would be surprised to discover that Eva had had the locks changed and she had just thrown the only front door key into the New York City sewer system.

Eva felt an immediate sense of relief.

Hailing a cab, she instructed the driver, "JFK please, and step on it."

4

It took only a few hours to fly to Miami.

Eva stepped outside the airport and greedily soaked in the sub-tropical heat. She hailed a cab and got in.

The cab driver didn't seem too happy after getting a good look.

Seeing that the cabbie was dubious, Eva threw a fifty dollar bill at him.

"Take me to the Fontainebleau Hotel, please," she requested. She had always wanted to stay at the Fontainebleau since it was the hotel used in the James Bond film, *Goldfinger*.

"Are you sure, lady? It costs a lot of money to stay there," he said, eyeing her pajama outfit.

Thankful that she was wearing sunglasses so the driver couldn't see how ridiculous she felt, Eva pulled her coat close about her. "Remember Howard Hughes wore pajamas during the day and he was the richest man in America."

"Really? Never heard of him," the driver replied as he pulled out into the traffic.

"Leonardo DiCaprio played him in a Martin Scorsese movie. You might have seen it."

"Oh yeah. He was that guy who peed in jars and kept them in his room." He glanced in the mirror at Eva.

"You don't do that, do ya lady?"

"Not lately."

"'Cause that is disgusting."

"I would have to agree. You don't have to keep looking back here. I'm not peeing on your seats."

The cabbie shook his head and muttered, "I get all kinds."

"What was that?"

"Nothing, ma'am. Be there soon. You've missed the rush hour."

Eva settled into the back seat and stared out the window.

Unlike New York with its cold gray shadows and dark alleys, Miami was flooded with brilliant sunlight that danced off glass skyscrapers. New York was a concrete jungle, but Miami was the Emerald City. Everywhere were vast expanses of deep turquoise water, white sails, expensive cars zooming here and there and sun-drenched mansions.

Suddenly it was too much for Eva. She felt overpowered by the immense glass city, which resembled a mirror. It made her feel raw inside, too exposed. "Listen," she said, throwing a hundred dollar bill into the front seat. "I've changed my mind. Get me out of here."

"Where you want to go?"

"I'm not sure. All this glass and sun. It's too hectic. I need something calmer."

"The Everglades?"

"God, no! The last thing I need is to encounter an alligator. I just got rid of one reptile in my life."

"Depends on what you're looking for. How about the Keys?"

That was a possibility. Things were slower in the Keys, weren't they? And she didn't know a soul in the Keys. Not a one.

"I just want to rest. Relax."

"Then Key Largo."

"Key Largo," murmured Eva, thinking of the Lauren Bacall and Humphrey Bogart movie. "Yes, take me there."

"Where in Key Largo?"

"Just a nice hotel."

"How nice?"

"A hotel with a nice pool. I like to swim."

"Motel okay?"

"No. I want a hotel. One that will have a concierge."

"You got more money?"

"YES! Just get me to Key Largo." Exhausted, Eva fell back against the seat. "Please, no more talk. Just drive."

Sulking, the driver changed lanes and made his way to Highway 1 heading for the Keys.

Two hours later, the driver stopped in front of an expensive chain hotel. "This okay, lady?"

Eva looked out the car window and nodded. "It will do for now." She paid the driver the exorbitant fare plus a two hundred dollar tip.

He no longer thought Eva was crazy, but merely eccentric. Rich people were never crazy, just different. She would make a great story for his family over dinner. Eva motioned for the hotel valet to open the cab door and help with various packages.

She had stopped at a mall on the way and had purchased some casual outfits. As soon as she stepped out of the cab, the silky breezes of the Keys enveloped her.

Eva took a deep breath.

The salty air smelled like home.

She felt the pain in her broken heart dull a little.

Eva no longer felt that she was going to die.

Perhaps with a little luck, she just might recover–even flourish.

CPSIA information can be obtained
at www.ICGtesting.com
Printed in the USA
LVHW111536110419
613828LV00001B/145/P